# PRAISE FOR *VINCENT AND ALICE AND ALICE*

"Shane Jones is brilliant."

    – Helen DeWitt, author of *The Last Samurai*

"This diaphanous novel beautifully elucidates the experience of living a life we're not sure how we got into, what we miss when parts of that life disappear, and the ever-present desire for what we don't have."

    – Melissa Broder, author of *The Pisces*

"In its intimate rendering of marriage, work, and a kind of archetypal American despair, *Vincent and Alice and Alice* feels fresh, raw, and funny, even in its most tender, saddest moments. It reads like a beautifully pinched nerve."

    – Kristen Iskandrian, author of *Motherest*

"*Vincent and Alice and Alice* contains my favorite combination: laugh-out-loud funny and knife-in-your-heart sad. Inventive, surprising, and tender. No one writes like Shane Jones."

    – Chelsea Hodson, author of *Tonight I'm Someone Else*

"Shane Jones is our 21st century Jane Bowles."

    – Catherine Lacey, author of *The Answers*

"*Vincent and Alice and Alice* has everything I've always loved about Shane's work—the vivid imaginative force field, the mordant humor—while marking a commanding departure. This is a novel of great intimacy and heart, one that held me close and moved me deeply."

    – Laura van den Berg, author of *The Third Hotel*

VINCENT AND ALICE AND ALICE

Tyrant Books
Via Piagge Marine 23
Sezze (LT) 04018
Italy

www.NYTyrant.com

ISBN: 978-0-9992186-7-9

First Edition

Book design by Adam Robinson
Cover design by Nicole Caputo

# VINCENT AND ALICE AND ALICE

A NOVEL BY

## SHANE JONES

# ALICE

# JUNE 1, 2037

He said he could show me my ideal gate. In my empty apartment I saw nothing, maybe the room became brighter, less filthy. In the light, he rolled a pill between his thumb and finger. It was the day after he left that I understood what, or who, he wanted me to see.

Now I'm alone and living in reality. It seems like few people are nowadays, but they're productive and happy. You would know more about the modern work force than I would. Is this what you wanted to hear?

# VINCENT

# JUNE 1, 2017

It's difficult to cook an exceptional scrambled egg because your brain thinks it's simple so you're overconfident and mess the whole thing up – dry them out, over-salt, drop an eggshell in the yolk. A lot can go wrong with eggs. And if you think about it, cooking eggs is a lot like living life. It's part of the adventure.

My marriage was an adventure, but it's not something I want to tell everyone about. It wouldn't make a good movie because the last forty-five minutes would be Alice and I silent in the kitchen, eggs twitching in a pan. Besides, I'm trying not to think about her anymore. I'm starting my life over.

But I've only known Alice as my life. You could say since the divorce I've been floating, suspended, in my days. I need to concentrate on what the world has to offer and move forward. So from here on out no more thinking about Alice.

Lately, I've been thinking about conference calls, which is when everyone lives in different places but you call a number and you're on the phone together. How the phone's fibers can withstand so many voices I'll never understand. Typically, two or three people do all the talking. It's never the smartest people. And if you want to be taken seriously you need to talk over everyone else. You need volume. The louder you are the more powerful you are.

When you arrive at work today shout, "Good morning!" and walk in exaggerated strides while staring intensely at your phone. If done correctly and with enough force you'll be left alone for hours.

I don't remember how long I wasn't paying attention on the conference call, but I woke up when I heard my name, *Vincent*. In my professional voice I said, "Please repeat."

Imagine thirty separate laughs rushing through a single hole and into your ear. Imagine working seventeen thousand hours in the same office. Imagine Alice saying she's leaving you and you know it's your fault.

I put the nail clippers back in the medicine cabinet. When I closed the door I was looking in the mirror.

"Vincent," my boss grumbled. "Your opinion?"

Certain images you remember forever. Every person has maybe ten slots to fill and you die and the slots, the images, flicker around your eyeballs before it's dark. What would I see? Dirty cubicle walls, Xerox light, neon screensavers, Mom and Dad driving, their sunny funeral, the podium incident, coworkers eating zucchini bread, Alice saying it's over, and me, standing at the bathroom mirror on a fucking conference call.

I'm not sure why, but what I did was laugh. Not laughing at the call itself, but at how I appeared in the mirror, and the idea I participated in something like a conference call. No one would be holding the phone if they knew it was their last day alive. Those who preach carpe diem repeat the same tasks their entire lives. Like a weekly conference call. But this was our job and we were doing it, and hanging on the line by its claws was the meaning of life – strange, terrible, and slipping.

My eyes were just watery, not crying over Alice, I told myself.

"Everything will be fine," I answered.

"What?" my boss replied, followed by more laughter.

I wasn't thinking about Alice.

"I'm on it," I continued.

My boss sneezed. "Um, elaborate?"

I placed my mouth an inch from the mirror and spoke into the phone, "Going forward I will implement synergy to achieve results."

I didn't want to be there, but I didn't want to be anywhere.

"Thank you," said my boss, relieved. "Thought we lost you there for a second. Everyone hear Vincent?"

My breath created egg-shaped fog on the mirror so I wrote my initials on the glass, and over my initials a question mark. Then I said goodnight and hung up.

# JUNE 2

Alice slept with someone else because I wanted her to be happy. People are like bags, and the more problems you have the more holes in your bag. Not like a *I want peanut butter but don't have any in the house* kind of problem. More like *Every 24 hours I lose another day so I'm closer to death.* Most people don't think about their end. Another hole in their bag. For Alice, the label of marriage was a hole constantly torn larger.

She often asked if she was destined to a life of unfulfillment. I'd say something like, "I'll work on it" to which she responded, "But what if this is your best?"

Here are some holes in my bag that I wrote into a PowerPoint slide because I was at work but didn't want to do any work:

- Alice
- Alice
- Fear of public speaking
- Alice
- Alice
- Alice
- Alice
- Alice
- Alice
- Alice

Before working from home I had the best cubicle in the office, located in a back corner where the cubicle walls were so high I was invisible. The light was always dim because I didn't have a window, but I didn't care. I had my own space that no one from where they sat could see into.

I called my spot the Zone. It felt far away from everyone else because it was. My coworkers would be discussing things like the weather, local crime, and meatball recipes in their open, middle-of-the-room cubicles and I didn't feel the need to respond because they didn't know if I was there. I was somehow in the office and not in the office, a body gone but living behind cubicle walls.

When my boss called my words slurred like I was waking from a dream. From what I recently read in Sarah's email they haven't filled the Zone yet, so there's the chance if I ever go back everything will be like before.

Along with conference calls I've been thinking about bodies. If you work an office job then you already know what I'm about to say. But I'm going to say it anyways because I need to concentrate on something besides Alice.

Bodies worsen if you work for the State like I do. Lots of workers dragging a leg, seemingly shoved by a version of their current self who wants nothing to do with squeezing through the security portal again. I'm not sure how they survive the day.

I rode the elevator one morning with a man who pressed an entire side of his face against the gold-colored doors and when they opened he muttered, "Lillian? Are you still with me?" and walked forward groping the air.

Eight hours of sitting is barbaric and in two hundred years everyone will agree. We're just not far enough in the future to understand what we're doing now. I forget who it was, but someone famous visited an office in the 60s and said it was like entering a crypt. She said the workplace crushed not only the individual, but the possibility for romantic love. I'm not entirely sure I agree.

Because I had a moment with Sarah and never told Alice. I liked Sarah because she would laugh when everyone else was serious. During a meeting my boss said he didn't want to be "the memo police" but if he had to, he would, and Sarah placed her hands over her face, pretending to rub her eyes. She's also the only non-white person in the entire office. Maybe the entire building. I think she keeps to herself because she understands what the place is. When my coworkers are at their worst she disappears.

Sarah and I were discussing how in ads featuring shirtless men the camera focuses on a man's abs because abs are the definition of sexy. Men don't care about women's abs, but everyone knows that. Sarah said something about Brad Pitt, and what I did randomly, trying to be funny I think, was lift my shirt up. I don't have abs, just a deflated goose-bumped space with black hair. I felt so dumb and began lowering my shirt. But what Sarah did was place her hand, flat, on my stomach.

It was a weird moment with no talking, standing next to Sarah in her padded swivel chair holding my shirt up. Everyone else was eating hot dogs but we were connecting. It lasted somewhere between five seconds and two minutes, I can't remember, time gets strange when you're far away from it.

Now I'm waiting for a conference call. And because I'm thinking about time, it's taking forever. I need to do more. I should drink eight glasses of water because everyone says it's important. I live alone and sit when I pee. I could stand now but I can't stop the habit. As a kid, I'd stand in my driveway with my eyes closed aimed at the sun and think so hard about being alive I'd have a panic attack. I can't do that anymore.

The reason I work from home now is because of the podium incident. Each May my boss gives a speech at the annual State workers picnic, sponsored by the Leaders who don't attend. The picnic is catered with deli meat, and all the Michelle's and Steve's and Emily's get wasted. There's a pavilion and a stage with a podium and the sun is always shining, making Doritos look beautiful in neon plastic bowls.

And every April my boss picks one employee from a hundred and fifty to introduce him in what is supposed to be a light roast with some brown-nosing at the end. He chooses by pinching the name from pieces of paper he swirls around inside a jumbo-sized cheese-puff bucket. Of course my name was drawn. Of course I didn't say I didn't want to do it. I spent three caffeinated weeks writing my speech. The night before, I couldn't sleep.

Steve, who wore an orange golf visor across his eyebrows shouted in my face, "Show the boss who's boss!" as I walked to the podium.

I had on my favorite suit jacket, the one I got married in, the one I never wore to work because it was a tailored summer suit and baggy pants are popular in my office. Besides, my office was a refrigerator. Did you know the number one complaint in an office is that the temperature is too cold? And can you guess what the second most common complaint is?

Everyone waited for me to speak. All those bodies in flip-flops and short sleeve button-ups gripping soggy paper plates of meat. My boss stood off to the side touching elbows with Sarah. I remember the air was cool and a few guys way in the back were playing cornhole on boards they had painted in the American flag. There was one cloud in the sky shaped like a moose. It fell apart as I thought about my life.

My face became flushed with rings of rising heat. My head was spinning, and the sky tilted until it became the grass and then the sky again. I tried imagining everyone in their underwear but I couldn't because they wore cargo shorts.

Then Steve chanted my name. In this world we never say no to Steve. But some just pretended to mouth the chant, like I did in school chorus, standing in the back and moving my lips. I fainted once during *Here Comes the Sun*. I walked from the auditorium and into the school and just before the nurse's office, I collapsed. Sprawled out on the floor with the silver line we had to walk single-file on and no one was near. I remember the fuzzy stars suffocating my face like a pillow and the janitor touching my face.

My boss stepped toward the podium and the chanting stopped. My boss should have known. I never really talked before, so why would I now? Why would I do a good job? It didn't make any sense and everyone knew it.

I couldn't read the speech because I was holding my wedding vows which had been in the summer suit for all these good, bad, whatever years. The speech was in the opposite side pocket, but I couldn't stop re-reading the vows.

What I did at the podium was smile and put my professional voice on. I made a joke about my boss drinking so much coffee that during his heart surgery they ran an IV to the nearest Dunkin Donuts. It was idiotic but everyone laughed. I don't think I had tears in my eyes when I made that joke. I don't think I was still thinking about Alice. Then the sky was the grass again and this time I couldn't right myself. My hands held the far corners of the podium but I was weak.

I told the blurry audience how my boss is the hardest working person I had ever met to no applause. No Steve power clapping in a deafening echo because my eyes rolled up in my head and the sound of a departing plane filled the air around me. I laughed at the disjointed moose in the sky and fainted. Losing my balance I took the podium with me; microphone, cord, water pitcher, plastic cups, off the stage we flew and toward the crowd and onto the grass where everything in my life collected in the dark.

Afterward, I sat in my car with the door open, supervised by paramedics, before being driven home by Sarah who owns a Mercedes even though we make the same salary. At a red light, she put her hand on my stomach and said everything would be fine. I pretended to be asleep.

Back home I received a call from my boss who said maybe some time off was a good idea. This is one tactic, out of many, when they want to fire you.

I should find a new way to live but my phone is ringing. Lately the conference calls have been getting shorter and less frequent, but more people are there. Maybe this time we'll break the record for voices on a shared line. A hundred? A thousand? *A million?* Could there be a conference call with all of America on it? What would that sound like? Would it be comforting to know everyone was in one place together? Could you pick out your spouse and say that you missed them? Could you ask about dying? Could you ask a stranger what it's like to live and get an honest answer? Through all the yelling and power grabs to be the loudest person in America could I find Alice and pull her through the voices and tell her that I loved her? Would America be on my side in weepy silence or would America just laugh?

After a conference call, I need to eat. Routine is important when you live alone because then you believe you're accomplishing something. I'm walking to the grocery store, about five minutes from my apartment, with the sun throbbing above in the blue sky. In the middle of the road a man in a suit is vomiting. On the other side someone is recording him. I never noticed this stuff before.

Because life is swirling circles of hell and Alice was the comforting pools between. Ugh, I'm not talking about her anymore. I need to concentrate on my future. You can't work on yourself if you're thinking about the past. Georgia O'Keeffe said that, I think. She narrowed her eyes at the future she wanted and said, "I'm going to make you my reality."

I want to be a healthy person but I buy junk food. There's the produce section, sure, but it's expensive and shrinking. The way the produce section is set-up now it's something you walk through, not shop in. One of the cashiers here told me that at least once a week someone is caught stealing bags of frozen shrimp that they immediately try and return without a receipt.

I do my shopping quickly.

A man in blood-red suspenders holding a Caesar salad is mouth-breathing down my neck. Sometimes I wonder why anyone exists. One theory is that Armageddon already happened, invisibly, years ago. I don't necessarily believe that, but hard to disagree if you're out grocery shopping.

Caesar Salad cuts the line. Forgetting something, looking at his phone, he moves from the line only to return seconds later and cut it again, his shoulder brushing past mine. He's big so he does whatever he wants. His left hand is in a cast, a tiny red heart smeared at the base of his thumb.

"Paper bag inside of a plastic bag," he demands, not looking up from his phone.

Everyone is thinking the same thing, but we won't do a thing, no way, not this group. If anyone was going to say something it would be a woman. Men are brave but only inside cars. We need someone like Alice. "Show a man who he truly is and he will change." A quote I like but it doesn't apply because a guy like this, taking time to study his receipt before leaving, so ready to pounce on a mistake, doesn't posses a sense of shame.

Back home I have a missed message. Too much time worrying about strangers with salads to realize my phone was ringing. Like Alice used to say, I need to be more aware and to be present. It's good advice in any situation and it's annoying because I'm unable to do it.

It's from my boss saying to come to the office first thing Monday morning for a meeting with Dorian Blood. I don't know anyone named Dorian Blood. Two weeks working from home and I'm going back, if only for a meeting, but it just goes to show, you don't really control anything. Dorian Blood can't be a real name and if it is what kind of head goes with it? Something oblong and bony. Someone with long fingernails and hazel eyes. I've never heard the name before. I would remember such a name if he worked for the State.

When people ask what I do for a living I say I work an office job and flutter my fingers on an imaginary keyboard. I don't know why I do this, but I do, grinning and typing on air. My job isn't interesting but sometimes if I'm talkative I'll say, "administrative work."

Because you can't tell someone you work for the State without them rolling their eyes. It's a detestable job. We're overpaid for bureaucratic paper pushing and the benefits are shocking to the point of evil. You put in thirty years and the pension package and best health insurance available in the country (Michelle calls it diamond level) follows you until death.

At 10am, if you drive by the building where I work, the one with thick streams of black gunk on the crystalized cement, you'll see smokers on the marble steps, or if it's windy, crouched and huddled between the bushes like gnomes. We have an absurd amount of free time, and time off, tripling what those in the private sector receive.

When we have a three day weekend with Monday off you're allowed to leave early on Friday, so most employees put in a request for Friday off completely, which is always approved. Wednesday is a breeze because you're thinking about the coming five days off, you can't concentrate on work if you even have work to do. On Thursday you can relax, come in a bit late, followed by a long lunch, sneak out early, and hey, another day off.

What's also common knowledge is that many jobs are created for the friends and family of the Leaders themselves. There's an office and job description involved, just no work.

And because many workers refuse to pay the fifteen dollars for monthly parking, they park in Center Square where there is a strict two hour limit. So every two hours, if not for a smoke break, they lethargically excuse themselves from their cubicles to move their car. During this break they make personal calls, nap, and buy potato chips.

I call my boss for details. He says he has none besides, "The Leaders picked you."

I follow up for more information and he does his nervous boss cough and says he's never had this request before, meaning from his boss, and to come with an open mind. He never talks like this. This is a man with a perfectly coifed "Greed is good" haircut. On his desk is a ceramic jar engraved with TERRORIST ASHES. He believes those on welfare should be drug-tested. I ask if this means working from home is over and he says of course, didn't his message say welcome back?

"I don't know what to say," I say.

What I've learned from working at the State: no sense of logic, karma, or linear narrative. You constantly feel like you will be fired even though all signs, like those older employees shuffling around you, point to you obtaining the coveted thirty year mark. That's the real reason people work a State job: free time in the present is nice; retirement at sixty is the real heaven.

Being home all the time is depressing, so I tell my boss, "I'm ready for anything" in the strongest conference-call voice in the world while driving my hand into a family-sized bag of tortilla chips. Without a future, no Alice, I'm ready for an adventure.

Dorian Blood. When I say the name there's a magnetic quality to the sound like I've met this person before. Dorian. *Blood.* I can't stop thinking about him, or her, and what this meeting means for my future. Possibly nothing, but maybe everything.

In an attempt to distract myself I go for a walk. I live neither in the city of A-ville or the suburbs, but somewhere between, the neighborhood of Pine Hills where two-family houses have fifteen feet of grassy separation on city lots, a sad scattering of trees for the corner homes. The streets are lined with parallel-parked cars, but some people have driveways. I live two miles from my office. If I walk two blocks over I can see the head of the building I work in, one shoulder filled with my coworkers, computers, and cubicle walls.

The weather tonight is a summer storm after a day of record-nearing heat. Elderly is holding his stuffed animal with spider-long arms and legs, curly blue hair and googly blue eyes. If this is surprising, it's not. Elderly is a street person well-known on the sidewalks of Pine Hills. I find him less troublesome than Caesar Salad. Only one has a stuffed animal named Millionaire. Only one seems destructive.

"Hey E. Nice night."

The thing about Elderly is he dislikes small talk, words to just fill spaces. But when it's important he talks in endless depth, going on and on about politics and current affairs. Just don't engage Elderly in chit-chat, he won't hesitate to walk away. Most people love to talk even if they don't like people, which is why they love to talk. Tonight he's got a bag of cans half as tall as him slung over his shoulder. Millionaire is positioned so the stuffed animal's hands appear to be holding the bag, his body hugging Elderly's chest.

The streetlamps click on for their thirty minutes, the breeze is sharp and exhilarating, and I say like it's no big deal that I have a meeting with Dorian Blood.

Elderly looks like James Baldwin, and when he hears the name Dorian Blood he raises his eyebrows and leans back on his heels. "The magician?"

"A work meeting. I'm going back to the office," I say.

"Why?"

It's a good question. I'm not sure working for nine years in an office has done me any favors except giving my life meaning to strangers. Because when you're asked, "What do you do?" you have to respond with your job, but if you're retired you just say, "I'm retired."

If I retired at forty years old I'd receive six thousand dollars a year beginning in 2037. I need thirty years total to reach the goal everyone in my office talks about daily – the diamond-flickering retirement package, seventy percent of your highest year salary. But the way it works, I need to reach year ten first to receive anything at all. I am less than a year away before I become vested into the best retirement package in the world.

"It's for a work meeting," I reiterate to Elderly. "I'm just not sure what, exactly."

He has Millionaire adjust the cans on his back. "Work meeting," repeats Elderly.

The outline of a person flashes in the distance under a tree then vanishes around the corner. I have a little Alice thought because it looked like her. I need to move on. Her side of things is a different experience than the one I had, I'm sure, but that's life. What you think is a highlight is a lowlight for the person you love.

Dad once told me his favorite experience with Mom was this white water rafting trip they took in the Adirondacks in the 70s, I forget the actual year, but it doesn't matter, they were young and adventurous. When he told this story he lit up, explaining how Mom beamed as they zigzagged down the river in the rapids, how he almost went over, how the buffet at the resort had all-you-can-eat crab legs and no one was pushy, no single wide-shouldered man stood there waiting for the refill. They got caught in a rainstorm while walking back and ran with mud painted up to their knees. What makes this story so memorable is how Mom felt about the trip. She hated it. It was the worst trip of her life. "Going for a walk," I tell Elderly who stares at me. "I'll let you know how the meeting goes." He doesn't care if I go for a walk. Elderly dislikes style, material goods, and leisurely activities. He definitely doesn't like work meetings. What I'm trying to say is that he's amazing.

When I'm walking at night like I am now into the areas of no street lights or glow from houses it feels like I'm being thrown forward into darkness with nothing to grab onto. I've read that people who have attempted suicide at the Golden Gate Bridge have experienced a similar feeling. But does anyone not suicidal feel this way? Everyone is so confident, so sure of themselves. I'll get there one day, maybe, just hard to imagine the future without Alice in it because Alice, as married to me, is always bleeding images from the past.

I like to cut through the park at night because of the stars. As a kid I could locate the most obscure constellations. I dominated the planetarium field trip. Tonight is overcast, the moon behind a wide band of gray clouds so it's difficult to locate a star or planet. Still, walking through a field alone in the dark with possible life above feels powerful.

Before leaving, I stand at the swing sets trying to find a star between the slight separation between clouds. Teenagers in hoodies are huddled on a nearby bench getting high. At the park exit men squatting under a streetlamp are spraying cleaner on a truck's tires, saying, "Yeah, Ronny boy, yeah," as the foam thickens. There's a sudden clearing in the sky. I trace the belt of Orion.

Another thing about Elderly is he lives in his car. I can see it in the distance as I walk home, a gold-colored 1995 Pontiac Bonneville which worsens each month and is rarely driven. When it won't start I help him push it from one side of the street to the other side every Tuesday and Thursday because of the parking rules. The Pontiac sits too low to the ground. It has no functioning headlights, the hood is dented so badly that when it rains it holds water, and one flat tire is covered with little crosses of black tape. The front bumper is missing, and so is a chunk of the car itself, a missing corner exposing an inch of blue washer fluid. Standing next to the car now, I can see Elderly is asleep in the driver's seat, which contains rips of white foam, crown-shaped, around his head.

From my porch I collect seltzer cans in a plastic bag. Tied tightly, I place the bag next to the driver's side tire. "Goodnight, E," I say, and he responds through sleep, "Night, V."

# JUNE 3

Time to buy a dog. I've previously planned this move in the direction of independence, it's just taken me a while to follow-through. A dog will keep me occupied until I meet Dorian Blood on Monday.

Months ago I was cleared by the animal shelter. It's interesting with so much dying the strict regulations we place on animal safety. When the volunteer inspected my apartment she went, "This it?" and moved in a stationary circle, clutching her clipboard.

I don't really have things. My apartment post-divorce is what considerate guests would call minimal. People talk like this now, and I don't really know what looks nice. Everything I purchase is blue or black.

There was some hesitation in my application because I imagine a single, nearly forty-year-old man fits the profile of someone who would burn an animal. When I told the volunteer I was divorced she said she understood because her boyfriend, Brandon, had recently dumped her for Crystal. Then she touched my wrist and approved my paperwork.

I didn't need to, but on the way down the stairs to the sidewalk I blurted out that I've loved animals ever since I was born, like, I came into the world loving animals so give me one to love now before it's too late.

The animal shelter is bright lights and barking dogs and worn leashes dangling from hooks. Two women sit on yellow chairs against the windows comforting cats. I've asked to walk Rudy. No one wants Rudy because he's disgusting. Also, in a world of Max's, Oreo's, and Winston's, he's Rudy.

Long brown fur that isn't curly, but knotted with dirt. Where it looks like he has long toenails growing from his paws it's filth-bundled hair, and around his eyes there's so much gunk it's permanently sleek. His left rear leg and part of his hindquarters has been shaven pig-pink because the leg, according to the volunteer, was coated in ticks when he was discovered in a dumpster behind a pool store.

Rudy is so undesirable. Probably doesn't have teeth. His breed is terrier mixed with a half-dozen others, who knows, no way anyone will adopt him before his day comes. They do a countdown until an animal is adopted, or not, and a dog like Rudy has little to no chance. Even before we go outside with everyone else testing out dogs, I decide he's for me.

There's a real sadness to the way he jumps, frightened by other dogs barking. When a man in the passenger seat of a convertible starts singing on a nearby road, Rudy cowers between my legs and I tell him, "I'll protect you from him," which is something you can only say truthfully to an animal.

When Dad was busy being a cop, Mom collected animals. She was lonely and filling her reality with things that had hearts. Don't believe what other people will say because plants don't work and fish don't count.

So we had nine cats, three dogs, four turtles, twin rabbits, three hamsters, a one-winged pigeon named Helio, and a squirrel, Bibb, who lived in the garage. Mom made Bibb a hammock above the workbench which Dad kept filled with peanuts. For their size, squirrels are skilled fighters. Is there a star constellation of a squirrel? If not, you could create one. For Bibb. That's what's so amazing about the world now – you can make anything up, and if you're confident in your stance some others will believe you, and if you have yourself and some others, it's all you need.

Alice never met my parents but the animal stuff she thought was so weird. She was careful about what she said about Mom and Dad and I don't blame her. How do you comment on two people who were dead from such an accident? Besides, if you don't grow up with animals as pets you tend to just eat them.

"Rudy?" says the volunteer at the counter. This one isn't as pleasant as the one who visited my apartment, this one is talking while eating chips. In the future everyone will be eating chips, constantly, all day and night.

A dog costs two hundred dollars.

The volunteer licks his fingers. "We can't understand why his tongue is bleeding."

"Right," I nod.

"He's eleven-years-old with a life expectancy of thirteen."

"Where do I sign?"

I imagine Rudy tossed slow motion like into a basement clouding with green gas, too late for my saving hands. The death syringe plunging into his fur and the black bag. My brain is killing Rudy. My imagination is powerful. On occasion, it has gotten me into trouble.

Alice said I was incapable of living in reality. She said I spent too much time in my head, which is impossible because my reality was Alice, planning our days together. We spent weekends in bed eating sushi, reading the first ten pages of novels, binging shows, sleeping to no clock, no rules, no guidelines, no sense of time. If my imagination did wander, it always included her.

Rudy comes out, dragged on his leash across the smooth-as-glass linoleum floor by an unaware volunteer until he reaches me and Rudy leaps, injected with sudden energy, his unclipped nails scratching my thighs.

How I landed my job when I turned thirty is all Alice, recommended by her brother-in-law who worked for a Leader. He said they were looking for "creative types." I no longer consider myself a creative type. My pants are so much bigger now. Imagine working thirty years so you can live twenty years.

The reason why my brother-in-law recommended me as a creative type was because I had a minor painting career before I met Alice. I'm not sure it was even a career, but people did buy them and it always surprised me. My paintings became boring around the time I settled into working an office job. Some new painters doing new things pushed me out of the way. The art world is a trap unless you have rich parents.

My parents had money, but not power money. They signed me up for lessons when I was ten and didn't say a thing when I brought home an oil painting the teacher herself had spent two hours on. She wanted to impress my parents so they thought I was excelling and would sign me up for more lessons. Mom and Dad were too smart for that. Where I had signed my name, in the lower right corner, were tall chunky blocks of smeared black paint and both of them ran their fingers lightly over the letters.

I started to feel embarrassed when Alice looked in on me, in the basement, dripping paint onto the canvas in uninspired ways. The shame of not selling paintings made me give up. Steve, on occasion, still calls me Hollywood because I once sold a painting for a thousand dollars to Scott Rudin in Los Angeles.

I'm not really sure where you bring a dog that has been living in a cage, and survived in a dumpster licking chlorine tablets, but my favorite park is twenty miles from my apartment, near Mom and Dad's old house.

Shortly after the divorce I drove to the house and asked the owner if I could see my childhood bedroom. This was the behavior of someone who had cracked, I don't deny this now, but I did then. I denied everything around me. Some hesitation, but the family felt sorry for me, because they let me in after discussing it in the kitchen.

I followed them through the living room and up a carpeted staircase and down a dim hallway with ascending school year portraits. Each room had a leather couch or leather chair like it was a requirement. A table at the end of the hallway held green candles, a mason jar full of pennies, and a picture of an elderly woman presenting a plate of spaghetti.

"Probably changed from when you lived here," said the mother who wore coffee-stained sweatpants and an Under Armour sweatshirt the color of dried blood.

"Yeah," I agreed. "There's a lot of leather."

My childhood bedroom was now a room for *Family Guy* memorabilia. A home is only walls, it doesn't matter how many years of your life you put into the space, it will eventually just become something else by someone else. But my childhood was in those walls. Too bad a house can't remember you. The mother said, leaning in the doorframe, that if you added up everything in the room it would be worth fifty thousand dollars, maybe more depending on the buyer.

"That's amazing," I said, and touched a doll of Stewie Griffin that was reclining in a mini leather chair.

Behind her, I could see her children in the hallway, watching us.

"No one will admit it," she continued, palm-packing Marlboros, "but *Family Guy* is better than *The Simpsons*."

◉

As I'm driving Rudy is sticking his head out the window with his blood-tongue hanging loose, drool streaming backwards into an SUV with the wipers on. He either doesn't care what anyone thinks, or he doesn't know how he looks so he can't care. Who was it that said animals have no interior life, that they can't recognize their own image in a mirror? How is that even provable? Either way, I wish I was more like Rudy.

I park the car. Neighbors spend hours blowing leaves from one house to another and telling their dogs to stop barking, who for years, don't stop barking. Cars get dirty so you have to clean them. Looking around, carrying Rudy in my arms until we reach the grass, this is what I see. I need to be more positive. Move into my future. But sometimes people just sit outside and watch traffic.

Two men in the baseball field are scratching lottery tickets as their kids wrestle under the monkey bars. I throw a tennis ball that Rudy runs toward, then right past, his head turning like the ball is stuck in the sky.

I have to carry him to the car he's so exhausted. I did a little running too. I'm so out of shape. I should start jogging like everyone else. Just run around the neighborhood until I can't think anymore.

I get in the back seat with Rudy on my lap snoring, a wet puddle from his mouth to my pants. He trembles, sprinting through the dream of what just happened, and I'm falling asleep too, the sun warm on our faces. Some people don't like dreams because they say they aren't real – those people shouldn't exist.

At home my boss calls again. He's never called me on the weekend before. He says for the Dorian Blood meeting to fast beforehand, no food after midnight tomorrow, get at least six hours of sleep, and don't do anything to, "compromise my normal routine come Monday morning."

I ignore how weird the request is, and instead look at Rudy in the kitchen who slobbers-up a half-gallon water dish then waddles to the corner and vomits.

"Okay," I finally respond.

"You'll be working here again like before, that's all I have right now," says my boss. "It's another program funded by the State."

"Same cubicle?"

"Steve put in a request for it, which I denied. See you Monday."

A rush of excitement comes over me knowing I'm going back to the Zone. Now if I can just get my life on track, no more Alice thoughts, I can relax and head towards retirement. Reaching ten years is so close then just two more decades, but then what? Alice has a massage license, a degree in biology, references from a dozen cafes and restaurants, a yoga certification, and works for a non-profit, RISSE, helping refugees. One location is right around the corner from my apartment. Sometimes on my way to the grocery store she'd be on the front lawn kicking a beach ball with kids who had survived bombs from their own government.

Rudy sleeps the rest of the night. I can't sleep, my mind piecing together what Dorian Blood looks like, what the meeting is about, where my life is going.

# JUNE 4

This veterinarian smells like weed. The adoption package includes a vet consultation but the bill, whatever it may be, is my responsibility. With the help of an assistant who appears incredibly young, maybe the veterinarian's son, they draw blood from Rudy's tick-scarred leg. When the vet places both hands on Rudy's sides and squeezes, moving from chest to pelvis, going, "*Huuummm… huuummm…huuummm*" Rudy coughs.

"Does that mean something?" I ask, concerned.

"Not necessarily," answers the assistant standing off to the side.

"Sounded like a man's cough."

"That's funny," says the vet, now looking at me but with his hands still around Rudy's ribs. "You ever see that *Seinfeld* episode?"

Compared to yesterday, Rudy looks worse under the lab lights. His fur is greasy and more gray than brown, his eyes droopy, his tail dangling between his legs like he has no control over it, like a strip of worn felt pinned on. With every trying-to-get-comfortable movement his black nails click against the metal table.

"I love TV," says the assistant, looking at his phone.

The vet puts on magnifying glasses, similar to what a dentist wears, and inspects Rudy's teeth and gums. He peers in, then pivots his head toward me while holding Rudy's jaw. "His tongue always like this?" The lenses in his glasses are rainbow-colored, and when he moves under the lights they become gasoline spills. The length of his pants, like the assistants, are about six inches too short.

"Yeah," I answer. "Always bleeding."

Rudy receives two shots which he has no reaction to. When they stick a thermometer in his ass he yawns.

"Good doggie," says the vet rubbing one floppy ear and peering at the thermometer that he holds up to the ceiling light.

"We'll know more when we test his blood," the assistant says confidently.

"But is he okay?"

"We'll call later," says the assistant.

"Should I be worried?"

"Please check-out with Sheryl," says the assistant.

In preparation for Dorian Blood I decide to buy matching pants, a dress shirt, tie, underwear, and socks. It's embarrassing that our culture is just to always be consuming, but a new outfit is what Alice did for me when I had something big coming up, like my last art show, or my 30th birthday party. I've never had friends really. But if your wife works with refugees who like to party, and you put them in an already crowded bar and they sing you happy birthday it feels like the whole world is with you.

I pull into the parking lot, leave Rudy in the car with the window open slightly, and walk toward the mall. I figure I can get everything in less than ten minutes. I have a vision: to go with my blue suit, some navy plaid socks, blue shirt, blue tie. What I refer to, amusing myself, as The Iceman.

A good trick in 9-to-5 living is to always be amusing yourself. Most people don't agree with this style of living. Alice was tired of it. One time, after watching television for hours where we didn't talk, I leaped from the couch and announced that I was Leg Wobble Man. My legs became a blur. I pleaded, "Come on, be Leg Wobble Man with me." Alice went into the bedroom, shut the door, and I didn't see her until the following morning, in the kitchen scooping coffee into the filter. I probably could have pulled Leg Wobble Man off when we were dating, not married for eight years.

The days severed me slowly from the person I loved. Dramatic, but it's true. I couldn't win against all those days transforming me from someone she cared about to someone she couldn't breathe with. Still, I sometimes think if she had been Leg Wobble Man with me it would have saved our marriage.

But there was this one time where she did something similar to Leg Wobble Man. We were eating dinner at her parent's house when she got into a fight with her father about the confederate flag. Residents had been putting them up more often, nailing them to trees, but still, nothing like what I see now. And what Alice did, as her father preached State rights with an embarrassing flourish of hand gestures, was gyrate her body from her seat at the head of the table. She moved into a mocking breakdance, fists rhythmically punching the air. No one said a word, and Alice didn't stop dancing until her father had left the room.

I miss that version of Alice. I read in a magazine that if you don't see the person you love for thirty consecutive days they disintegrate. I haven't seen Alice in one hundred and seventy eight days. That means all through space she is suspended bone dust, floating arteries, unraveling veins.

But I still see her as I put together my Iceman outfit, judging my choices outside the changing room, saying, "The shirt is too big, spend more and buy something you actually like."

The reason I don't have things in my apartment is because they reminded me of her. I crammed the grassy space between curb and sidewalk with hand-painted side tables, pastel-colored yoga mats, a fifty-pound juicer, health tonics in little amber jars, faded Anthropologie comforters, a dwarf-sized Buddha statue with a chipped nose, black beads, piles of self-help books bookmarked with pieces of paper containing inspirational quotes. Ten minutes later, a couple in a truck with confederate flag bumper stickers picked through everything before finally deciding to take it all. "God bless!" said the woman in the passenger seat, waving enthusiastically as they drove away.

I'm leaving the cool mall air and into the sick heat of the day. So far this summer has been nothing but constant storms. One hour it's clear and hot, the next rolling-in thunder clouds. I hate the local news, but according to them we're going to break a record.

Walking into the parking lot, a miniature lake of rippling waves is next to my car on the pavement directly under the back window. I can't explain it, but that's what it looks like in this blinding sunshine. Why did I park so far away? I guess I just don't care about a close spot at the mall. The back window appears a shade darker compared to the other windows. Maybe it's the light in the sky, a cloud passing over. I half-jog. I don't see Rudy.

It's not a miniature lake of rippling waves – the back window appeared a shade darker because its been smashed out. My feet crunch onto a circle of broken glass. I open the door. Where Rudy should be, on the back seat drooling, looking up at me with his blood-tongue hanging out, a note states there's a special place for people like me. If there's any karma in this world, the note continues, my fate will be to remain in a hot car with the windows sealed for eternity. At the margin in bold red marker it says 85 degrees translates to 119 degrees. Drive yourself straight to hell, ends the note.

I drive home with the back window a gaping mouth of jagged clear teeth. A driver honks, in my periphery I can see him waving, but I look forward gripping the wheel. People in A-ville are real heroes. It's not even that hot out. I wasn't in the mall for that long. I left the window open.

My phone rings. I answer by hitting speaker and tossing it onto the passenger seat. It's the veterinarian who sounds like he's holding in smoke.

"Hey there. Kidney failure," he says, then exhales through, "without proper meds Ralph has two weeks."

"Rudy," I correct him.

"That's it."

With Elderly's help we tape flyers to the mall entrances asking for Rudy's return, his medical condition exemplified by skull and crossbones clipart. I didn't have a picture of Rudy, so I drew one. On Elderly's urging, I offer a cash reward. The designing, printing, driving, putting them up, takes less than two hours. I put the last flyer on a corvette parked diagonally across two spots.

Elderly, while driving home with all the windows down (he said he wants to achieve a cross breeze) tells me a man living alone dies ten years earlier than a man married. I thank him for his help. He says he appreciates the cans I've been putting next to his car and drumbeats the dashboard. We have a good relationship but I feel sick.

I turn my alarm off and start a pot of coffee just before sunrise. Outside my window, a squirrel in a tree is eating a congealed slice of pizza. Tomorrow I'm going to meet Dorian Blood.

# JUNE 5

Before walking to work I check on Elderly, who is asleep with Millionaire draped over his chest. The car's interior is mostly trash, a weedwacker wet with grass clippings rests across the back seat. When Elderly is feeling good he likes to trim the edges around the park and nearby abandoned properties. Two homes are on my block. Millionaire, strapped to his waist with a rope-belt, helps him. In the front passenger seat are two Rudy fliers and on top of them a gold cross on a silver chain. On a torn piece of paper he's written *I'm religious now* and taped it with what looks like peanut-butter to the glovebox.

I own a car and walk to work. My coworkers think my throat will be slashed for walking two miles, through what they consider a violent neighborhood splattered in graffiti, but it's just poor people.

Back on floor fourteen, everyone says in chilling unison, "Welcome back, Vincent." Hung on the outside of my corner cubicle wall is a banner: "Welcome back, Vincent!"

On the snacking table is a box of donuts and I'm allowed first pick. Nothing has changed since the podium incident. The copier is jammed, the plastic plants are gigantic, it smells like Windex, and Francesca has thumbtacked a sign on the wall – *Clean Me After You Use Me* – with a blurry picture of the breakroom microwave.

"Thank you," I say, "it's nice to be back."

The Zone has a huge computer monitor, comically large for the work I do, that's new. Then the typical stuff – pinned memos to the cubicle walls, filing cabinets, ceramic pen holder, IBM printer, uncomfortable blue office chair, phone directory that needs updating, too much gray desk space, and a thick area rug weaved in black and brown square design purchased by Alice. What hasn't changed is that I can still hear my coworkers, and they can't see me.

Once, before working from home when I was in the Zone, Emily brought her daughter in and afterward Michelle said, "Little bitch doesn't know what life will do to her." At the time I thought that was a really tough thing to say about a seven-year-old, but after Alice left me I kind of understood. Even Michelle has her moments.

Today she's telling us that a pig can have an orgasm for thirty minutes. I ignore the conversation and instead log into my employee account with five hundred emails. None of them matter because here if you don't do a specific job it just flows to the next person. Because I have to click on them individually it takes ten minutes to do my deleting. Then I'm done with my work. I have nothing to do until my meeting.

Eventually, he came to hate his creation. His name was Robert Propst, which is the perfect name for someone who would design the first cubicle. His 1960s blueprint allowed workers a comfortable space to work in, and for the first time ever, privacy. But once the companies figured out they could shrink the cubicles to save money, and add more workers to increase profits, and shorten the walls so the supervisors could spy, that was the end of the dream. Years after his design was implemented he visited an office like mine and stood in the entranceway, turning his chin over the expanse of cubicle walls, bald heads and hairdos on rounded shoulders, everyone able to hear everyone else breathing. "This is monolithic insanity," Robert Propst said to the proud supervisor beside him. "I've created something that hurts people."

I'm pacing just outside my boss's office near the water cooler. Dad said being early shows respect but he was wrong. I arrived forty five minutes early to the dentist once and the receptionist said while photocopying my insurance card (best dental in the country, diamond level) "Did you know being early is just as inconvenient as being late?" Alice said it was true. Being early throws people off their track. They love routine. It's why everything they do, important or not, is on a schedule and screen.

"Vincent, get in here," says my boss.

This boss is not the person who hired me. I was hired by the new Leaders at the time because I was a creative type who could write press releases. Then the old Leaders regained power through the elections and rehired the old employees back, like Steve and Michelle, but for some reason I wasn't let go. I am one of a handful, from hundreds, who weren't fired. That's why working in the Zone is so special and odd – I have the most secluded spot and my boss and the higher-ups and Leaders working across the street in the Dome don't know what to do with me.

The Dorian Blood meeting is on floor twenty, which I didn't know was in use. My boss says it was empty for years, formerly used by lawyers during the 2012 coup, a complicated story involving multiple back-stabbings, an affair between two opposing Leaders, and a smashed electrical box resulting in an office blackout. I ask for more details and my boss shakes his head. "I don't know much," he says. "As usual, I'm just the messenger."

This only makes the Dorian Blood meeting more eerie because it's not my boss in control but a Leader I've never met. This is how the world works now. Entire rooms of people you'll never meet are making decisions about your life.

He says Dorian Blood is the head of a new work productivity program, and that he feels guilty because of what happened at the annual picnic. He was asked what employee fits a certain profile and supplied my name. A ten percent raise included in participating in the program will drastically affect the percentage of my retirement, he says while grinning, and I can't help but smile too.

"Good luck," he says.

"Thank you."

"One more thing."

"Absolutely," I say in my professional voice.

"Francesca's birthday."

If there's any future consistent with the now, it's an office birthday, the same as the previous, continuing forever inside an endless streak of office buildings. When a birthday is planned everyone who doesn't have a birthday contributes. You sign your name next to a responsibility and this sheet travels from desk-to-desk in an unmarked manila folder. Because I'm the last to see the list I'm responsible for the most difficult task, the cupcakes.

"And one more thing," says my boss turning to his computer.

"Of course."

"She likes the desserts from a diner. Is that even possible?"

The professional me, continuing: "Anything is."

On my way to floor twenty I share the elevator with a woman in a black shawl. She's not Alice level attractive, that's impossible, but has that quality some posses who work in an office environment where they appear shockingly clean. I'm speaking in a way Alice would disapprove of. I could never look that clean because men need money to look that clean. "Nice shawl," I say. Shawl Lady turns and faces the wall until the elevator stops at floor eighteen and she side steps out. With no one watching, I shrug.

The elevator opens and I walk onto blue carpet and face a sign:

---

PER / SUITE 2037 / BLOOD

---

After using the wall phone outside a locked glass door, I'm greeted by two men with professional voices and professional smiles. They're college age young with a combination of confidence and calmness I can't relate to. Their gingham shirts are slim fit, their purple ties knitted, their fingernails attentively cared for, not bitten like mine. One says, "Nice to meet you" while vigorously shaking my hand, and I feel like I did that day at the podium, that at any minute the recessed ceiling lights could become the floor.

The Iceman isn't succeeding. But I follow the two men, maintaining some distance between, trying to calm myself down, unable to remember my mantra. My future is coming for me? My future is mine? As we enter an office space full of light, I'm thinking about Alice again.

From her point of view the reason our marriage ended wasn't because I couldn't fulfill her sexually, but I stopped connecting. She said I wasn't *there* with her mentally because I was either commuting to work, at work, coming home from work, or dead-eyed from having sat for eight hours at work. Sundays were spent preparing for work. I soon realized something that horrified me: I slept 9-to-5 and worked 9-to-5.

Besides, she was so busy at RISSE, sometimes working twelve hour shifts, which I admired and made me look like I was accomplishing nothing. How can you compare teaching a Syrian refugee

45

resume etiquette with printing a twenty foot banner: WELCOME TO THE EASTER EGGSTRAVAGANZA?

Whatever she thought or still thinks, I was there, with her. Which I realize now was part of the problem, how, after giving up painting, I was stifling her and the marriage. I became too much of having nothing to do but Alice. That makes sense now. I was jealous of her work and it wasn't fair. But I was there. I tried.

I brought her dinner at the refugee center once, and in the common area everyone was kneeling on neon-blue rugs. There was a glass compass on the floor and Alice was next to it, praying. I didn't say anything. It was so powerful with everyone submitting to what they thought God was that I couldn't move.

"A rattlesnake can live a year without eating."

I'm in a huge room outside a corner office with the two men now typing on their phones. The corner office door is open but no one is visible, only a voice coming from inside. My stomach growls this disgusting high-pitched bubbling that disappears in a whimper.

"I've heard so many good things," continues the voice.

In office meetings you morph into a language and set of body movements if you're aware of it or not, it doesn't matter, but it's not you in the meeting. Some people are better at this than others. They are built for the changing. I never speak in meetings, let the big dogs roam special, but years ago my boss caught me laughing. I was having "one of those days." Everyone stopped talking and I said toward the window, "You know none of this matters." I wasn't trying to be difficult, it's just sometimes you forget where you are and you say something real.

"Vincent, come in." An arm, most likely connected to the voice, is waving at me from the open door.

The office I walk into contains a framed Ronald Reagan illustration leaning against a freshly painted white wall with stacked cardboard boxes around it, an oval shaped wooden desk with an open MacBook, and next to a set of large windows, sitting on the air conditioning unit, a shallow cardboard box with broken glass. It smells like cigarettes and mouthwash. There's more, but this is what sticks out as I move into the space and take a seat across from Dorian Blood.

I ask if he recently moved in.

"Yes, about twenty minutes ago," he says, looking into the larger office I just came from. "The reason I mentioned the rattlesnake not eating for a year is a metaphor for energy conservation, routine, and discipline. In case you were wondering."

His graying hair combed backwards contains gel. His skin is clear and unblemished around narrow pale-green eyes. White cables are tangled in a mess around his laptop. Maybe he really did just arrive, he's not making it up. Outside, the two employees are unpacking cardboard boxes like the ones in here and filling two center cubicles with printers, telephones, black lamps, cords, manila folders, laptops, and glossy stacks of copy paper. The morning light is half-filtered by the blinds set at various uncaring levels, and I'm sitting in a chair across from a person named Dorian Blood.

He could be thirty five or fifty, it's hard to tell with the graying hair but tailored suit and youthful skin. And he's thin, but fit from what I imagine is a habitual lunchtime walk and morning push-ups. "Straight off the bat," he says with his fingers making a peace sign. "What are the two biggest complaints about State workers?"

I'm lightheaded from not eating and sweating. "That the work is dull and the jobs are a waste of taxpayers dollars."

He looks pleased as he settles back in his chair, a silver Cross pen seesawing between his fingers. "Couldn't have said it better myself. Perfect, just perfect. I see why Frank picked you. Now, what if I told you I can change that."

Sometimes I do this thing where I stick my bottom lip out and nod. I did this a lot toward the end of the marriage, when Alice was packing her belongings in those shit-orange Home Depot boxes. She would say, "You're bottom lipping me again" when I didn't know how to respond to, "We don't connect anymore."

And I bottom lip now with Dorian because I don't know how to respond to the claim he can make office jobs exciting and worthwhile. My office isn't necessary. You could erase my department and the world would continue without a glitch. I'm not just saying this. I know it.

Because when there was a major shake-up in the Dome, the coup, I was given the position of Supervisor which I didn't want. This was two years after I started and what I learned, having access to the office budget, is that we could be liquidated and nothing would change except saving half a million dollars. Another office, the printing warehouse uptown could easily do the work we were doing with the addition of interns (unpaid college seniors who are worked until cynical). But I didn't say anything, because if I did I would have been firing myself.

"Let me back up," says Dorian. He loosens his tie, very similar to the blue one I'm wearing, and rolls up his sleeves revealing a gold watch with what appears to be a thin black wire dangling from the back, a charger, I can't tell what exactly. "So this is the third state we've been to this year," he says. "Sometimes I get carried away during the screening process because of the success we've been having. Increased worker productivity, improved quality of life, taxpayer savings. The program is technically and originally called Patrol for Everyday Repetition. PER, for short, is what we call it now. Follow?"

"What?"

"Vincent," smiles Dorian. "We're going to change your life."

I lean back in my chair attempting to give the impression that I'm not completely dumbfounded. I try and access the conference call version of myself but he's not here. The air is suddenly difficult to breathe. I've never been one to adapt well to these situations, but I've lived in them for so much of my life. Maybe the coming years won't be so dull, so hard, though, if Dorian Blood is telling the truth. But that's impossible.

"I follow," I lie.

"Are you lying?"

"I'd like to hear more."

Dorian smiles and his teeth are so white they appear fake. "It requires training," he continues, "but you shouldn't have a problem. I've gone over your file." He leans forward. "PER is a way of life, a routine and a process and a discipline in order to live a fulfilling existence while being a productive worker. This, you're smart, means more money for citizens, more beach vacations, new cars, televisions, family gatherings, you know, things that make people happy. But the main goal is not only increased productivity, but bringing joy to the workplace. It's something that has never been done before."

I imagine Elderly's reaction when I tell him about this, his eyes widening to cartoonish width. I imagine his stunned expression, and, in this vision, I'm nodding at Dorian Blood and becoming increasingly interested.

Dorian casually says, "Give us a chance and you'll see what we're about. Everyone successfully engaged has experienced a more pleasant, more positive, daily existence. No one deserves to get hired at a well paying job and a month later be depressed. Isn't it sad how people stay in these jobs until retirement just because it's a so-called good job?"

"That's true," I say. "It is sad."

"PER alleviates that."

I let everything sink in and bottom lip some more. I don't really have a choice. If I say no, I have to explain why I declined to my boss, which could jeopardize my position in the office, possibly sending me back home to work. No more Zone. No more increased retirement package. I could be sent back home forever, and there's too much Alice still in there because Alice is impossible to erase. I said I wanted a future, and here it is, presenting itself.

"Okay," I say, not entirely convinced. "I'll try it."

"Fantastic." He slides a binder from a corner of the desk on his side, and across the desk to me. "Here's the questionnaire and script for the blood test, to be done after you leave here. The process can be challenging, but Vincent, it's going to change your perspective on everything." He rubs his hands together. "Before you go, can I ask you a personal question?"

"Sure," I say, and my heart races, thinking of Alice, seeing her running down an endless hallway.

"Are you happy?"

On the shiny white binder is an illustration of a waterfall flowing out of a computer, the name PER below in delicate script entwined in black ink mist.

"I'm not sure happiness is part of the deal," I say, not looking up from the illustration that I'm touching with my finger.

"The deal?"

"You know," I say turning my palms up on the binder. "In life?"

"The answer a depressed person would give. No more conference calls. How does that sound? Pretty good?"

I tell Dorian that conference calls are soul sucking vortexes and each one kills me a little more.

"We've treated two hundred people, possibly more," he continues, smiling. "The success rate is something I'm very proud of, probably talk too much about, but I'm sorry, it's just what I do. You'll still be working 9-to-5, but adjustments to your routine will take place and it won't necessarily *feel* like you're working 9-to-5. This will become clearer after the training. What's important is that you are willing, which is how the other participants started."

"And they're happy?"

"The program showed them their ideal life, so I'd say so."

I flip through the binder with hundreds of questions typed on heavy paper, each page with the PER waterfall logo. "But what's in this for you?"

Dorian stands so I stand too, signaling the end of our meeting. He shakes my hand by pulling my arm toward his chest and says, "Vincent, your happiness is my reward."

At the LabCorp across the street I fill four vials of blood as dark clouds form a thunderstorm. A nurse whose hairline starts in the middle of her head says I have big veins while handing me a sugar cookie. Next to me is a pregnant woman reclined, flanked by two paramedics and a man, the father I presume, in a denim jacket with Bugs Bunny on the back. I take a huge bite from the cookie and it starts to rain.

I walk home excited and lightheaded to complete the paperwork. People are running because it's raining, and those waiting for the bus are crowded under the little metal station with red trim. I like those who just walk in the rain with no umbrella. There's something spiritual about it even though I couldn't tell why. I just think the slower a person walks in a downpour the better they are.

On my way home I pass the refugee center. It recently had a fire. A third of the roof is black char exposing a room once used for cooking classes, where Alice showed me how to make babaghanoush. The front door is boarded up and graffiti under the windows, most likely something evil stated, has been covered with black paint in the shape of a ship's hull.

Back in my apartment, I sit on my bed and flip through the binder before grabbing my laptop. For all the questions in the binder there's no explanation on what, exactly, I'm going to be doing. I type "Patrol for Everyday Repetition" "Dorian Blood" and "PER" into various combinations.

It takes a while because the word Blood really throws things off. I'm shown numerous pictures of bleeding gums. Participants must be sworn not to publicly say a thing about PER, but eventually I find a crinkled article turned into a PDF, ten pages long, written by Kate Helms and Dorian Blood. It was published fifteen years ago in a sociology journal called SCATZ FORUM on the benefits of, get this, "extreme daily routine."

A majority of the text is blacked out. But there's a chart with ascending numbers on one page, and on another page black rectangles labeled "Reality" and "Ideal Gate," attached antenna-like to a floating head in a work cubicle. On another page there's an illustration of a watch with a tail snaked around a wrist and a nearby potted plant with all surrounding text blacked out. The chart and pictures are childlike in their simplicity. On the last page is the waterfall logo. The caption beneath the mist says that, "PER activates the subconscious dream of life."

I have no idea what any of this means. I have no idea what I've gotten myself into. I am filled with panic and excitement and fear. I email the article to myself then slam the laptop shut.

*Shit.* I forgot to order cupcakes for Francesca's birthday. Immense drama in the office tomorrow. *Fuck.* During the divorce I forgot strawberry pie for Emily and for three days no one talked to me. No real loss, just hours of cubicle whispers I knew were about me. But I want to start fresh in these PER office days.

The questionnaire is divided into two sections: Professional and Personal. Some sections have already been computer completed – thirty nine years old, a reliable worker for nine years, no political affiliation, less than a year removed from being vested in the retirement system. A page printed of a PowerPoint slide using a bamboo textured backdrop has a scale from strongly disagree to strongly agree:

- You respond to e-mails and dislike a crowded inbox.
- Your home environment could be described as minimal.
- You are rarely distracted by fantasies and ideas.
- Others do not influence your actions.
- A book is preferable to a social event.
- Real world objects are the focus of your dreams.
- Your emotions control you more than you control them.
- You often contemplate the reason for human existence.

There's more questions like this until the personal questions on height, weight, diet, and routine. The routine questions are detailed down to the exact minute inside a typical hour. For example, from 7 am to 8 am what minutes do I consume (the paper's wording, not mine) brushing my teeth, showering, opening the refrigerator, checking my phone. There's also a question, mostly a blank page with small text, with the dimensions of a typical one bedroom apartment as an empty box asking how many steps I take inside this hour where the steps are located, *draw them if possible.*

Also, before bed, what minute *if it can be accurately stated* do I fall asleep on? I answer to the best of my ability. In my new life, I am honest. In my new life, I throw myself into the world of PER.

I'm in bed re-reading the Blood article. I've completed the paper-work, agreeing not to discuss the program with anyone or post anything about it online. Outside it smells like thunder, a breeze coming from my bedroom window that's open an inch. I feel a real sense of pride having completed the paperwork – exhausting for sure – but so much better than a conference call, which is what I think when my phone rings. Sometimes when I'm forced to look at a screen I want to throw up.

"Hi there. Sorry to bother you so late sir," says a shaky voice, "but I've found your dog."

I sit up and a bag of Doritos falls off the bed. My apartment has reached far beyond sad-bachelor level depressing, very little in here, such moody colors, dirty clothes everywhere, a permanent male stank. "Where is he?" When I speak, my voice echoes a little.

"I found a flyer," says the voice.

"Can I ask whose calling?"

In the background a car passes by.

"You can."

Someone behind the voice is saying to hurry up.

I walk to the front windows facing the street. There are three windows total and two don't open because the landlord used bargain priced paint. This is something all landlords do, no exceptions. When there's a sale they buy in bulk and use the same stuff forever. The basement here is littered with self-adhesive Spanish floor tiles, plastic plumbing fixtures, gallons of Fabuloso floor cleaner, and columns of paint cans customers outright rejected after they were mixed. I look out the window. Elderly is on the sidewalk, next to the Pontiac parked in its usual spot, holding a phone. Elderly doesn't own a phone.

"Who is this?" I ask.

I should have seen this coming. He likes to call the flyers of anything with a reward. With his lifestyle, I don't blame him. I've seen him tear a flyer for a missing cat from a telephone pole and later that same day pluck a flyer off a postal box for a missing turtle. Although I'm not sure how he would actually receive the money without the pet.

"Tom Ruddles," says Elderly. "Says something about a cash reward? I require that first."

He's bent over and inside the open driver's side window, and a young kid on the sidewalk with his arm extended is asking for his phone back. Behind the kid are three girls in high-waisted jeans, thumbing their phone's glowing screens. The lawns behind them rise and ooze a strange darkness, the grass moving in the breeze.

Elderly walks around the back of his car and grabs one of the flyers off the passenger seat. The three girls point dramatically at the boy who takes one step forward before peering into the car. "You're such a good boy, aren't you a good boy, that's right, you're a good boy," baby-talks Elderly, now walking back around the trunk and holding the flyer up to the boy.

"Tom," I say, excitedly knocking on the window. "I'll be right out with the money."

"*Cluck cluck*," goes Elderly, looking up at my apartment. "Busted."

I put on the one pair of jeans I own, bought by Alice, and leave my apartment, which desperately needs to be vacuumed, there's dirt everywhere. Did you know a new vacuum cleaner costs the same as a new dog?

Outside my apartment there's a concrete staircase built into the hill, like all the houses on my block, and when Elderly sees me coming down, then crossing the street while waving at him, he throws the phone at the boy and jumps in his car. I've never seen him actually drive the Pontiac besides the occasional lucky burst to get to the other side of the street, so I'm not surprised when the engine doesn't start, his head craned over the twisting key. I open the passenger door that makes a rusty hinge kind of sound, and I imagine it falling off, crumbling into red sand when I shut the door.

"Sorry, V," he says dejected and leaning back. "You ever get bored and do something weird? That's what I do with the flyers."

"It was a good try," I tell him.

"You think so?"

"Absolutely."

I sit on the soft maroon-colored seat and consider severe work routine and ideal gates and a work program obsessed with increasing work productivity but tied to an individual's happiness, this program I'm intrigued by because I have nothing else to be intrigued by. Maybe my office life really will improve, become something else entirely. I wonder if any of my coworkers will be in the PER program. Maybe Emily?

She wears purple everyday and her cubicle walls are covered with pictures of horses printed from the work printer. That's how much she loves them. Emily seems so depressed – slumped shoulders, forced smile, calling her husband who doesn't answer twice a day, too much sitting, too much cafeteria food – but on Friday she's always insisting we can't be unhappy on a Friday. But you can be unhappy on any day you want. Even a Saturday. This is a pretty innocuous thing, I know, Emily should be able to say whatever she wants, it's not hurting anyone, but what makes it so sad, and what I relate to, I think, is knowing via Steve who remodeled her kitchen, that Emily never has weekend plans. Her body in her cubicle on Friday afternoon is her body on her couch come Saturday evening.

"E, I need to buy cupcakes," I say, taking my car keys from my pocket. "Can I buy you dinner?"

The first time I met him he was installing handmade stop signs. Alice and I had finished moving the last of our belongings from the U-Haul when my brother-in-law dropped a table on the ramp. Hundreds of half inch glass cubes scattered down the street and toward Elderly who, glaring at us, gripped a wooden mallet.

"Sorry about that," I said, extending my hand. "I'm Vincent. You live in that house?"

"I live in that car," he said. "1995 Pontiac Bonneville. Best vehicle this country ever produced. And I own it." He walked over and pressed the mallet against the window.

He wore blue gym shorts, no shirt, and his calves resembled torched pepperoni. From the neck up he was a hippie Santa Claus balding, a mad-man with wisps of white hair and a vacant stare. Still, there was something strangely handsome about him, in his scars – it felt like he had lived through some rich past experiences, had seen some real life shit, which I immediately admired.

"Nothing to apologize for the way these cars, too many cars in this world, drive down this street. Better they get a flat from the glass then kill the family dog," said Elderly. "That's what happens, you know. They drive too fast, they kill the family dog. Ends the family. You look surprised. But there's no coming back from that, especially for a child. Politicians ignore me, that's why I'm doing my own signs. They kill the family dog? You're down, you're done."

The signs were torn Home Depot lawn bags, white house paint, and wooden stakes of various heights. Each one read SLOW

DRIVE NOW FUCK. He had hammered them into the grassy space between curb and sidewalk down the entire block. They would be taken down later, violently, by a police officer with sleeve tattoos as the sun fell but the air didn't cool – Elderly asleep in his car, myself questioning my new neighborhood from the front windows I couldn't open.

On the drive to the 76 diner, an establishment with a thin metal statue of George Washington standing in a rowboat, Elderly rolls down his window, and finger counts every other house saying, "Poor people love the flag."

I've always wondered about this, so I ask, "Where do they even buy them?"

"Buy them? They've had them in their family for generations. It means something to them."

"Yeah? Like what?"

Elderly looks at me like I'm crazy. "That they aren't poor."

The 76 caters to the wizened on fixed incomes who enjoy huge portions for a low price. They consider this tremendous value because they can stretch their leftovers out over several meals, eating through the stomach cramps by envisioning money not spent. The air conditioning is either never on because the regulars have complained enough to keep it off, or it's on chilling blast because other regulars have complained enough on the comment cards to keep it on. Tonight it's on frozen blast. Brown cardigans, herringbone caps, black shawls, and pilling sweaters are everywhere.

In a corner booth, Elderly glances at the menu before clapping it shut and telling the waitress, at our table for the drink order, that he'll have the clams casino.

"Turkey something," I add.

"And two Bud heavies."

Sitting across from Elderly, who is joyful and talkative now that he's receiving a meal, downing his first beer in two gulps, I have nothing to talk to him about besides PER, which feels wrong because I also realize, watching him shimmy uncomfortably on the booth's engulfing leather seat, that I know nothing about him as a person, even though I've seen him weekly, almost daily, for ten years. I'm not sure why I never took him out to eat before. I've given him food on occasion, typically on a holiday along with extra cans, but never out to eat. I've always assumed he was in Vietnam and not to bring it up.

"Clams have no head," he says flippantly. "They're just a flat heart cleaning the ocean." He starts on his second beer. "Millions of clams stolen from the ocean only to go down a human throat until shat back." He touches the hanging ceiling light, a Tiffany style knock-off with gold and avocado colors, and it sways. "Just because it's there doesn't mean you have to eat it," he adds.

"But you just ordered clams," I smirk. "It's what you're about to eat."

"I ordered *clams casino*," he says offended. "There's a difference."

"What difference?"

"Casino," he replies.

"I had my meeting with Dorian Blood," I say sipping water. "He runs a program called PER, stands for Patrol for Everyday Repetition. Increases office productivity by showing the workers their ideal life. You believe what our taxes are paying for?"

"Yeah, sounds religious," Elderly says drinking his third beer. The beer is served in short amber glasses, same as the water, and it's difficult to gauge just how much he's consuming, but who cares, he lives in a fucking car.

He becomes relaxed, shoulders slumped, voice deepening as he taps the rim of the glass. "These companies are always on the hunt for new ways to save money, especially if it's taxpayer money, real nice for the Leaders who don't have to do a thing but write the check. Been this way since the first office. Why do you think they came up with the cubicle? With technology I'm sure the possibilities are pretty endless. And cheap. And terrifying." He smiles. "What will we be doing to each other in the year 2037?"

"The logo is a computer screen with a waterfall coming out of it."

"I've seen that in Tehran," he says, stacking the jelly packets into a miniature wall he immediately knocks down with a quick whack of his knife.

"You lived in Tehran?"

Elderly closes his eyes and rests his head on the table. The skin of his skull appears paper thin.

The warm plate of clams casino is slid across the table and bumps him awake. The waitress apologies but she meant to do it.

"In the late 70s I was in Syria for a few months, but Iran was my home while setting up the phone systems." Elderly says this like it's no big deal, spooning out clams covered in breadcrumbs, bacon, and chives. I don't even know his actual name, age, if he's been married or has kids. "That's where they had that image you described, well, not exactly, but this very 70s screen with liquid pouring out. But it was the art style at the time, this combination of old world caves and sand and temples mixed with American pop art, very futuristic in Tehran. We messed it up. We messed up the future. Do you know anything about Tehran? Now it's offices and God. Doesn't matter your thoughts on the Shah, just the images of Tehran then, the blue and orange box cars, the bell bottoms and long black hair, the street sales with spices and sterling silver. I could go on. There's never been a place so quickly accelerating into the future as the past so desperately clung on."

He's on his last clam and stops again, entering these moments where he realizes, I think, he's saying too much, it's not like him. Maybe he just wants me to keep buying drinks, he needs his past to come flowing from him.

So I order a hot fudge sundae and three more amber glasses of beer to the disdain of the waitress who believes, correctly, we are poor tippers.

"Alice worked at the refugee center on Johnston," I say reluctantly. "She taught the refugees how to apply for a job. She's doing something similar in Chicago. A bigger position. Maybe has the title of Director. I hate when people have titles."

"Who?"

"My ex-wife."

Elderly wipes his face with the back of his hand. "Why would she help people who don't need it?"

Sitting near us are two old people who have been arguing since we arrived. They remind me of Alice and I when we couldn't communicate if it wasn't an argument. When you're in love all language is interesting. Now there's a dispute over what to leave for the tip. The woman says, "Just because you're stupid doesn't mean it's my fault" and the man, running his finger down the receipt, placidly throws a hard candy no-look into her blouse.

"Because," I say turning back to Elderly, "RISSE helps refugees in this country. They go because they want help."

"That's what I said," he responds, holding up one grubby finger toward the annoyed waitress, then pointing literally down and into his empty glass with the same finger. "They don't *need* your help, they just want it."

The waitress slides me the check. Even with my order of three dozen cupcakes, the Freedom Cupcake which is a specialty here, it's less than a hundred bucks. Elderly went to the bathroom, and now he's walking back out, slipping his shirt over his head.

"I was employed by AT&T," he continues, pleasantly surprised I've bought him another beer with cash – he slides into the booth, the cushion exhaling air. He takes a sip before pushing the glass towards me. "The phone systems were these headsets the employees wore and beeped when they completed quotas. Thinking back, this kind of office, so American, is what Iran really hated. I mean, not everyone, just the most passionate, which is what matters if you want a revolution. It wasn't about a decline in morals or women running around showing tits or smoking opium to "Gold Dust Woman," nah, it was the corporations creeping in, the profits connected to happiness. Didn't help that the Shah looked like a Hollywood actor playing a CEO. Sounds so simple now but the beep worked as a Pavlov's dog kind of thing, kind of putting the worker into a daze, I don't know. I don't know anything else. Just installed the wiring. Just these workers were proficient and left work happy, even if still in the daze. Anyway, the system was pulled after the revolution. People want freedom but they don't know what to do with it, look what happened, look what's happening here. I was gone after Nida was arrested. Hey-o I'm drunk." His head flops forward, seemingly unhinged before springing back up.

"Nida?"

"My first wife," he slurs, head swaying.

"You're married?"

"Was."

"What happened?"

"She was kidnapped by the Shah during a women's protest." He stops, and tears form in his wrinkled face as the boxes of cupcakes arrive by the waitress who doesn't make eye-contact or say a word.

Outside, we pass an idling car with the old couple facing their windshield and screaming. The woman's chin is frothed with her own spit. The man is shaking his head so fast that he has become smeared. Sometimes other people are hell. Sometimes it's nice to have someone to argue with.

I drive Elderly back to his home, the 1995 Pontiac Bonneville, lit-up under a streetlamp.

I walk in the dark holding cupcakes for Francesca. Up the concrete steps and into my apartment to vacuum and consider my happiness.

# JUNE 6

Shawl Lady is in the elevator again. Today her hair is dyed red, the only part visible because her face is wrapped tight with the shawl which extends downward to green flats. She shuffles over when I enter. "Good morning. Beautiful day out there." I figure everything else in my life is becoming out-of-control so be friendly, be present. Again she turns and faces the wall, inches from it, until I exit on floor fourteen.

After settling into the Zone I realize I've forgotten the cupcakes. It's not even nine and Emily says out loud, seemingly to no one that she can't wait to eat. The cupcake party is at eleven. Emily repeats herself. The way people communicate from cubicles is they talk louder than usual while facing their computer and someone in a different cubicle responds. One time Steve said, "Spare ribs are the best" and no one responded. I don't know why I remember such a thing, but I do. Same thing here happens to Emily.

I don't have time to drive home so I'm going to ruin everyone's day. I should get some work done before my orientation with Dorian at ten, but I have none, hooray. I delete two emails previously deleted, previously sent to the trash folder.

Finally, Steve says that he's hungry too. He says that when the weather gets cooler he'll bring in venison for everyone.

On floor twenty I'm greeted by the employees who were setting up cubicles the day before. Today I learn their names: Fang Lu and Billy Krol.

Fang Lu has black spikes for hair and wears rectangular black framed glasses with below patches of cheekbone acne. He's young and surprisingly fit and well-dressed, probably has an entire closet of J. Crew. I can't relate to him in the slightest. Billy Krol is taller with a thick trimmed beard, thinning hair, but also wears glasses and appears physically strong, like he played college rugby or just previously enjoyed being large. They seem to share the same wardrobe. I decide to like Billy Krol more and direct all my questions his way.

I follow them to the two center cubicles in the room. Hanging loose on their wrists are the type of gold watch Dorian wore yesterday with the black tail attached to the back and dangling from the skin. I'm told to sit sideways, my arm resting on the desk of a recently cleaned cubicle that is lemon-scented and sticky.

"Try to relax," says Billy Krol.

"This will be easy," says Fang Lu.

My packet is reviewed by Fang Lu reading the Professional section and Billy Krol tackling the Personal. They are the perfect working halves in the program, skimming through my paperwork with admirable ease.

"Both parents deceased?" asks Billy Krol with no sense of compassion whatsoever, not glancing up from my paperwork.

"That's right," I answer.

"You still drive?"

"I usually walk to work."

"Friends? Living with anyone? Staying in contact with exes?"

"No, completely alone."

"Great," says Fang Lu, initialing the bottom right corner of each page. "A perfect candidate. Fifteen day training will be a breeze. Then your gate."

"Yeah?"

"Your ideal gate, what Dorian discussed."

Billy Krol sticks an electrode to my left temple, then runs a white cord into his laptop on the other side of the desk on which my arm is resting. I can't see the screen but it's beeping. The laptop Fang Lu types on also beeps and neither him or Billy Krol look up.

Occasionally nodding at Fang Lu, Billy Krol types non-stop until he's satisfied with whatever readout he gets. He rips off the electrode then does the opposite temple. The computer beeps louder as the internal fan clicks on. Billy Krol burps and excuses himself. I have so many reservations about this process that my head is spinning, but I can't say no. I let them do whatever they want now so I can move forward later.

Deep into silent minutes where Fang Lu and Billy Krol complete paperwork and continue typing on their laptops, I ask what I have to do, exactly, for the program to be successful. I vaguely remember what Dorian said and what I read from the article, but I don't have any specifics. I won't get an answer, but I want to say something because the silence, only a beeping computer, is too awkward.

I mention the article I found yesterday and neither seems surprised, they just continue their work. Maybe I should tell them how Rudy was kidnapped, but nobody wants this story. If you tell anyone this story they might put their hand on your shoulder or give you a hug, socially forced to respond. A story like this puts people on edge because they don't know how to genuinely react, unless they can relate because they too have a kidnapped dog story, but then what are you left with? Two people complaining about zero dogs. So, I pinpoint my question – I ask what they're responsible for in PER.

"We monitor your gate," Fang Lu says flatly, "so it runs smoothly in accordance with your work output."

I turn to Billy Krol. "Does it hurt?"

Before he can answer, Dorian comes walking from his office in the same suit as yesterday, a thin gray blazer now creased like he spent the night sleeping on the floor. On his way towards us he kicks an empty box across the room and into the blinds. He has the body movements of a teenager and the head of a middle aged man. He's chewing something, and takes a second to finish before asking me to come into his office.

"Do you know the story of the amusement park ride and America?"

The office is the same as yesterday, even the box of broken glass is still here. The way the sunlight from the office windows is hitting it reminds me of the glass in the parking lot, the taking of Rudy. I want to ask about it, but how do you ask about a box of glass without receiving a fucked-up answer? On his desk, a half-eaten PowerBar lays glistening on a Post-it note.

I want to appear intelligent so I say, "The amusement park ride story, yeah, it's Tocqueville," without having ever read Tocqueville.

I don't know where it came from, but Dorian places a small white box on the table, similar to something you'd see at an Apple store. He leans back in his chair, stretches his long arms, and pops forward, sitting up straight. The office air conditioning is losing its fight against the sun. Everyone looks forward to summer but summer is disgusting. Fall is the best season. You meet a person who says summer is their favorite season, just walk away. Dorian waits for the janitor to finish emptying his recycling bin.

"The story is the office life, the 9-to-5 life, is like an amusement park ride. When you go on it, you think it's only temporary, a section of your life, because that's how our minds are wired." He pauses, letting what he just said sink in. What a professional. "But when you're on the ride for years, the repetition of work, hour after hour, becomes second nature, a funnel of sorts that consumes your life. Vincent, stay with me, because this is crucial. It's more than just going to work for eight hours, it's the getting ready for work, buying a car to travel to work, buying clothes for work, talking about work when you're at the family reunion, paying rent with the money you make at work, preparing your lunch for work, going to sleep and dreaming about work. Your Christmas presents are khaki pants. What should be part of your life consumes your life, infects how you truly want to live, how you *should* be living. What happens through this drudgery is that you don't understand anymore how you truly wanted to live in the first place. It just goes away from you." He moves his hand outward from his heart while wiggling his fingers. "Now some people never go on the ride. Street people, the homeless, the mentally ill, the chronically unemployed –"

Another janitor comes into the room, wearing a shirt that says YEARS OF ABUSE to empty the trash and Dorian waits again, nudging the white box forward.

"These people we never let near those on the ride. Because they're already so far gone inside their own minds, their own fantasies, and we don't want them infecting the ride, our boring reality. Society runs on the ride, no matter the misery, which is the current problem – productivity has slowed because the ride has slowed, it's no longer worthwhile or fun or interesting and it's getting worse. How will things be in twenty years?"

I don't answer.

"The program allows you to stay on the ride while physically interacting with the life you've always wanted. Stay with me. We turn the routine into something positive. You are both one of those on the ride and one of those off the ride. You'll be working, but it won't *feel* like you're working." He sneezes. "Excuse me. Not Tocqueville. Bill Hicks."

"I still don't get it."

"Baby steps, Vincent."

Inside the box is a gold watch with a black tail. Between my fingers the tail is worm-thin, a cord about an inch long with a clear bead at the end. I want to flick it, but Dorian can tell and says not to. He walks around the desk and snaps the watch onto my wrist, the glass face flashing with the waterfall logo. Looking up to Dorian like a child to a parent, I ask what the black tail does. "It's for monitoring purposes," he says, and points out the door in the direction of Fang Lu and Billy Krol who wave enthusiastically from their cubicles.

Now we're walking to the far end of the building, through vacant office space between hallways, cabinets with missing drawers tilted over, windows half-covered with chipped blinds, the blue carpet littered with paperclips, crumpled paper, gum wrappers, dead leaves, chewed pen caps, extension cords and power strips unplugged. It smells like the air in here has been recycled for years.

If my office building is shaped like a robot standing into the sky, then we enter the far right shoulder. Dorian holds his ID against a card reader which flickers from red to green. We go through the doorway and turn right.

"We have the whole floor," says Dorian, who for a second walks like he's straddling a horse. He massages his lower back with his forearm. The gel in his hair is losing its hold, little hairs curling up in the back. "It's like a maze up here because the building went through three architects in five years. It's all messed up."

Into another office we pass by a series of floor-to-ceiling glass dividers and on the opposite side – the effect appears to be mirrored – are twenty rows of cubicles endlessly miniaturizing forever. I want to be horrified, but I'm impressed.

"New data entry department," says Dorian, slapping the glass but still walking. "Ever see anything like it?"

"No."

"I told you PER is going to change the world."

The sun is so bright it doesn't matter that the blinds are drawn as we enter the last possible room on floor twenty. A chestnut colored leather couch with brass rivets and a bulky TV on a dusty moveable stand are the only items in this small depressing space. The couch I've seen before, same style as those across the street in the Dome, positioned in long curving rows outside the Leader's chambers. The TV stand I've also seen. When Leaders want to loop a video of themselves talking, have everyone on their lunch break be forced to pass their moving mouths, they place them strategically around the plaza. It's creepy but you get used to it.

I'm told by Dorian to watch a thirty five minute orientation video. With this time frame, I'll take the elevator to my floor just in time to experience my coworkers end-of-the-world disappointment because they don't have cupcakes.

Getting comfortable on the couch I ask, "Is that VHS?"

Dorian, crouched in front of the TV stand, like what I remember in elementary school, turns his head. There are wrinkles along his cheek bone. His eyes gleam. "Not exactly," he says.

The video begins on a solid lime-green screen, the sunlight from the windows now dulled but still brightening the room. I lay on the couch as instructed and Dorian pushes both sides of my gold watch inward. Nothing happens. No waterfall image or ascending numbers or twitching of the tail, all of which I imagine because this process is either a dream or a nightmare.

"Wait," I say, again looking up to Dorian who places a soothing hand on my shoulder. He has this magnetic quality where you just follow everything he says. His touch is – this is embarrassing – it's motherly.

White text scrolls up the lime-green screen which I recognize as the *Know the Laws* governing handbook each State employee receives when hired. You sign an oath before you work. But no one reads the entire thing. I didn't. It's extremely important that you read the entire thing. I remember my boss intensely grabbing the book off my desk after my first week and tearing the last perforated page out, telling me it doesn't matter, just sign.

"What exactly is going to happen here?" I ask, frightened. "I need to know before we go any further." I say this second part in my professional voice because I want results.

Dorian steps backward then crouches. "Well, in fifteen days you'll be living in the world your subconscious has suppressed for your entire adult life. Is that so difficult to understand?"

"Of course," I say in more of an exhale than speech. "It's impossible sounding."

"Not from our perspective. You look at the results we've had elsewhere. I've seen the changes firsthand. Think about the world, Vincent, who is running the world right now. We're both imagining the same face. Anything is possible, it's a big chaotic mix and it's time to experience joy. I told you to give us a chance and here you are, ready." He stands and then walks to the TV, blocking the screen. "The vision, unique to you, is your gate. It will reveal itself as an image at first, which you can't disrupt, then slowly be integrated into your reality. Remember the amusement park ride?"

I nod. "Hicks."

"You'll be working in rigid patterns, brain maps, to position you both on the ride and off the ride." He speaks with such confidence it's hard not to just go along. I somehow understand what I'm hearing and also have no idea what's happening. "Through the training, the repetition schedule, your gate will overlap then blanket your reality," he continues soothingly. "Imagine a clear film covering the physical radius of your life, ten miles or so. The film is what you deserve, what you desire, everything else, the trips to the grocery store, paying your phone bill, brushing your teeth, changing your car's oil, stubbing your toe, working with your coworkers, it's all still visible and you'll interact with it, but the film is the happiness."

"How will I know what's real and what isn't?"

"We get that one a lot, but at this stage in your life does it matter?"

After the lime-green screen, the video begins on a locked shot of a sprawling office layout, hundreds of cubicle walls with barely visible heads. A host, a woman in a lab coat with wavy red hair, big white sneakers, enters from the left and speaks directly into the camera with a Scottish accent about the decrease in worker production as blooming boxes expand then shrink to her left and right, showing workers sleeping under desks, arguing on phone calls, and scrolling social media for days. One box shows a short interaction between two coworkers at the water cooler. The host turns to listen:

> Hey Kev, what do you call a two hour lunch for a State worker?
> I don't know, Mike, what?
> Mid-morning break!

A clip art frown face momentarily presets over the paused inter-action until frosting away. It's silly, it's meant to lighten the mood, I think, but it doesn't really work, I'm still on edge. The host smiles until the box disappears.

She walks the endless cubicle rows, down a center gray aisle holding a notarized legal document as she explains how it's difficult to fire a State worker with union protection, even if they're use-less. An adjacent line graph, which also appears in a blooming box next to her, depicts the loss of taxpayer dollars from these workers. Another video clip on the opposite side of her, in another box, shows workers happy and productive in the workplace and most importantly, at home. All the workers in this clip have one physical characteristic in common: they're wearing the gold watch. Another line-graph shows how PER workers are not only happy, but how they save taxpayer dollars, increasing revenue for the State.

"The work life you're experiencing right now," she says, "doesn't have to feel so meaningless."

She reaches the end of the office – more clips of dead-eyed workers, taxpayer money-loss charts popping out then disappear-ing – and turns around facing the camera. She is looking right at me. She is telling me how to live.

The floor goes transparent and falls away to a powder-blue sky and a vibrant farm-like field she now stands on. Electric green trees are on the horizon and in the foreground white butterflies. She steps backwards into the digital background of nature. Still trying to get comfortable on the couch I whisper, "What the fuck."

"Everything you've always wanted is possible," says the host walk-ing through the field and toward the trees. "It just depends on what you are able to access, what part of your mind can bring up what it is you want, what you want to see, how you want to live."

The screen is dimming. "Thousands of societal and cultural entities are against you but we're here to help you." The screen is fading to light gray. "What you want is what you deserve. Thank you for letting us help you." The screen goes dark.

The next section of the video concentrates on two success stories: Lucy from Topeka, Kansas, and Aidan from Atlanta, Georgia. Each one tells their story from a brightly lit hotel room interlaced with documentary style footage of their 9-to-5 jobs performing data entry: frequenting the grocery store, running on a treadmill, eating three meals, then sleeping. Incredibly rigid and boring. But Lucy and Aidan say they've never been happier.

"Routine as second nature," says Aidan, "is exactly that. It helped me open my gate. I didn't believe it at first, but here I am, not depressed anymore. I wake up smiling."

I make a *pfffffittt* sound and the couch squeaks.

Aidan might live in a basement apartment walking distance to his job but what he experiences, according to his testimony is a three story home with granite counter tops, stainless steel appliances, basement gym, and a wall-mounted 65 inch television. Of course none of this is shown in the video, only Aidan walking to work and being at work. Lucy is more extreme. She lives with her handicapped mother in a 1940s ranch-style home and a front lawn filled with garden gnomes. Lucy bathes her mother daily and spoon feeds her pureed foods but tells the host in the brightly lit hotel room that she has won the lottery, drives a Lexus, and spends her time at the beach working on her tan. Again, the video just shows Lucy walking around her neighborhood, wearing a headset and typing at work, eating dinner with her mother who takes her meals on a hospital bed stationed in the living room adjacent to the kitchen. Aidan and Lucy never stop smiling.

◉

The TV screen becomes faint in the light coming through the blinds, so I sit up and lean forward. I fold my arms across my chest because it's cold, the AC never stops, it's increasing with the sun. I think about shouting out the door to Dorian for a blanket.

Five more testimonials. Some of them speak like they're confessing to cops. But everyone has the same thing in common: no spouse, no children, totally alone, like me. It feels like a video to attract cult members. I like to consider myself a good judge of character, and all these people are genuinely happy. They're not actors, I'm sure of it. Italic white text moves up the screen over Aidan gripping an Employee of the Month plaque, before disappearing into the top of the screen:

*IMAGINE*
*A WORK LIFE*
*EXPERIENCED*
*AS YOUR IDEAL LIFE*

An anti-testimonial is given by a tiny man in denim with a sunken chest, Johnny Star, who speaks with a lateral lisp on the dangers of not participating in PER. Working a 9-to-5 without the program will end in ruin, according to Star, who documents his mental collapse while speaking into his lap. After working eighteen years at COMPAQ, he randomly left work one day because half his computer screen, the words, numbers, and color coded spreadsheet cells were falling off his screen. When he looked at his keyboard it was upside down, and the left side, the same side of his screen that was crumbling, was dripping into the floor. Even when he stood and looked around the office the entire left side of his vision – half cubicles, half printers, half coffee pot, half stacked boxes of paper, half coworkers in suits – was melting into the floor. He felt a tremendous tightening in his chest, but not on the side of his heart. He was sweating so much a coworker asked him before he left if he had been doing sit-ups in his cubicle. In the video Johnny Star laughs and it makes me want to cry. Outside, he didn't want people cascading into the sidewalk so he shuffled forward while looking only at their feet, the whole world above trickling down his left eye. It took him nine hours to walk home. Later, when everything in his apartment was still dripping down his left side, he called an ambulance.

This section of the video is very effective. There is something deeply compelling about Johnny Star. I don't want to end up like him. I want to see what Aidan and Lucy saw. It ends with the host saying that what happened to Johnny Star is what happens when reality becomes too much and how you, meaning me, need a break. PER is the break.

Back inside the office now buzzing with activity, the host sits on a couch flanked by tall green plants. The couch is metallic blue. The plants are identical to the illustration from the Blood article I found online. To her left another box opens, this one neon-yellow with white font:

1. Do not confront the gate about its plausibility.
2. Do not question humans inside the gate.
3. Do not control the gate.
4. Let the gate guide you.
5. Do not attempt to escape the gate.
6. Documenting the gate by video or photo is prohibited.

The screen changes to lime-green as my gold watch lights-up with the waterfall logo:

```
WELCOME TO PER
DON'T ESCAPE
FROM MONOTONY
EMBRACE IT
```

Dorian yanks the blinds open. I squint. It's immensely bright outside, the surrounding skyscrapers once productive agency buildings in the 70s are all windows outside these windows producing a feeling of surrounding eternal sunshine. It takes a second to figure out where I am and to understand what I just viewed. Dorian seems pleased. Maybe he reads something in my face, it's hard to tell, but I feel proud not scared. He's smiling.

"Well?" he asks.

"Okay," I say. "I'm ready."

Fang Lu and Billy Krol connect me to more electrodes.

I am given a second packet detailing how my life should be lived in accordance to PER. When I'll be waking up, what to eat, how to exercise, how to act in public situations like the grocery store or shopping, what time to arrive at work, what work I'll be doing at my computer (data entry, surveys State workers hand out by the thousands at town halls, county fairs, job forums) is listed on twenty cream-colored pages.

Dorian says the 9-to-5 routine is the pendulum swinging low, and slowly, and further and further outward it swings into my morning routine and eventually my home life. He scoops the air back-and-forth, wider and wider. He looks like a performance artist of sorts, a mad dancer, a professional who has said all this before and is now a bit bored. Fang Lu and Billy Krol ignore him, but I can't stop watching.

I bring up how my dog was stolen, isn't that what the video considers "outside interference?"

I picture Rudy struggling for air as he walks the interstate behind the mall, then collapsing in a wooden clearing, and the trees bending inward. Strangely, I view this as viewing myself sitting in the Zone, seeing Rudy and the trees on my computer screen over my own shoulder. Dorian and Fang and Billy are right, I will have no problem with the training. I see birds swooping down from branches to inspect Rudy's body. A rat, standing on its back legs, scratches at Rudy's stomach, and I think some animals should be able to bring other animals back to life, but God lacked creativity.

Dorian assures me it will all become second nature, a blank slate, he says, walking backward toward the windows and wind-milling his right arm into a circle. Remember the film, the subconscious, off the ride and on the ride, he says. His lips are thin and pink, his skin today nearly transparent. A full circle, he says.

I'm walking to the Zone through a quiet office, typically this is the best type of office, but not now, no way, dog house for me, yes sir. It's not that no one is here, everyone is, but they've heard me coming from the elevator, my ID card scanning, so they've stopped discussing how I forgot the cupcakes. They will never forget I forgot the cupcakes. I enter the Zone.

After the first batch of data entry tasks, entering numbers 1-5 into the PER System, which has the waterfall logo in the bottom right corner, I hear Michelle and Steve talking in his cubicle followed by her ringtone, which is Native American wind flutes. My name is whispered. Steve burps. Michelle laughs. Steve farts.

Michelle laughs some more. I ignore it all and work the PER System.

Francesca sits directly outside my boss's office, a kind of gate keeper who answers the phone, watches YouTube videos of soldier family reunions, and energetically makes coffee throughout the day. A tireless worker, eternally producing, never complaining, who is paid the least.

As State employees our salaries are available online to the public, but it's not really for the public. Letting Steve or Michelle know they make more than Francesca adds an additional level of power to the structure. I've passed by their computers before and on their screens are hundreds of salaries. You get to see where you rank, what your worth is, in the wasteful eyes of the State.

Pouring myself a cup of coffee, which I'm not entitled to because I'm not in the coffee club after working from home – my name heavily scratched out in blue pen on the club chart tracking who purchases bulk coffee – I wish Francesca a happy birthday and explain how I left the cupcakes at home. I'll bring them tomorrow, I say.

"Thank you," she says, watching me sip coffee as I walk to the windows overlooking the plaza, much closer now that I'm not on floor twenty.

A man sunbathing on a roof throws a Frisbee to a poodle who nearly runs off the edge before biting it and bringing it back. The man, not looking, does the same, this second throw a bit harder, and the dog does the same, even closer to the ledge, but biting it and bringing it back to its owner.

"Good coffee," I tell Francesca. I've always felt like coffee is a drug so you should buy the best, and what I'm drinking is the cheapest coffee available. I'm shocked how people with good salaries will put the poorest quality of goods into their bodies. My boss makes $175,000 a year and spends pennies per cup, complaining of headaches and acid reflux, his stomach gurgling over what he is telling you during meetings.

"Folgers," says Francesca. "Master blend."

"Great," I say.

"The best," she adds.

In the break room one morning there were two pieces of paper, one taped on the refrigerator, the other on the cabinet above the sink:

> If you would like to join the COFFEE CLUB!
> please see FRANCESCA. Otherwise, please DO NOT
> "HELP YOURSELF" to coffee. THANK YOU!!!!!!!!!!!!!!

With the way Francesca is glaring at me I have no doubts this sign will return by day's end. Only Wednesday and I'm on the outs. At least I have the Zone to relax into, my PER training, enter my ideal gate which, standing at the locked windows, listening to Francesca smack gum, this guy on the rooftop now taking his underwear off, seems impossible. Still, I'm moving forward with my life. I'm excited by what could happen to me.

"Nice day out," I say, trying to sound pleasant. "Warm, but nice."

"It was a nice day on 9/11 too," replies Francesca.

I'm cleaning my bathroom, which I haven't done in months. This isn't a quick clean, but a deep clean where, with a wet-paper-towel-covered finger I dig up gray gunk between toilet and floor. This is an activity encouraged by Dorian because I think the idea is to kind of lose yourself in a bland project, just like my new 9-to-5 schedule will do to me, creating a blank slate so my gate will open.

After two laps around the bowl I find a hair. An Alice hair. How did it exist back there for so long? I think it's no big deal and throw it away. But while brushing my teeth, guess what, the hair is in the sink. How's that possible? So I turn on both the hot and cold water and flush it far away from me and any memories of Alice at this sink brushing her hair. Bye, see ya, I'm off to my future now.

Sometimes I imagine Alice doing something simple, like walking across the living room and smiling at me before sitting down with a bag of chips and I'm sick all through my body, nostalgia is worse than fire. Alice blowing out birthday candles while looking up at me. Alice at the beach squatting in the ocean to pee. Alice telling me to just leave her alone. It wasn't always this way.

Before we got married, we spent a weekend in the Adirondacks and then on Monday afternoon decided to drive to Brooklyn for a house party. We had no hotel, no place to stay, we just went. I remember how exciting it was driving from the mountains and later across the Brooklyn Bridge framed with lights. This could be one of my final images, along with my boss drunk and sleeping in the bathroom stall, because I can still feel the way the air, those lights, felt while driving hundreds of miles with the windows down.

The house party was a Halloween party thrown in June, which made things interesting because no one had easy access to a costume. This was the point. The host had a sense of humor. Alice and I went as a bruise, black and blue clothing purchased cheaply at a Wal-Mart. I wore black sweatpants and an itchy turtleneck and Alice, she still looked amazing, wore a pear-shaped shiny blue dress found on the maternity clearance rack.

"A-ville sucks," said a man with socks all over his body. Socks on his feet, socks on his hands, socks rubber-banded on his ears, socks hot-glued to his nipples. "Have you seen the condom?"

We spent most of the party alone in a back bedroom. We would have never done this years into the marriage because everything about me was still interesting. We joked about moving in together and even drunk it didn't feel like a joke. It felt like the only necessary thing to do. We were both living alone and could barely make rent. I don't remember much else about the party besides the sock kissed the condom. I think we passed out mid-conversation, in a heap, on the host's bed. I woke up hungover and excited.

"If you're living together it doesn't make sense not to get married."

I hate to admit it, but this advice came from my boss and it made sense. I couldn't stop thinking about being married to Alice and proposed in the kitchen. We didn't need a big production. I was ringless and she said yes. Years later she said I never proposed to her.

I'm being sentimental again but I don't care. When we had plans it was in bed together, reading, watching shows off my laptop, going out for Chinese. For dessert Alice would ask if I wanted "The Holy Trinity" and I'd say yes, of course, who wouldn't want such a thing, and she'd come back with Doritos, diet Coke, and a Snickers. Then everything became routine. We didn't need anything else until we did. For some reason, the music we listened to back then became embarrassing later on.

After our wedding she didn't want to have sex. With me. She looked up from her reclined spot on the couch, the spot I'm in now, with an expression saying we were more friends than newlyweds. I don't disagree with this now – we never had what you'd consider a sensual relationship. Because I'm not a sensual person, even though I would tell Alice that I was. But it became more and more important to her, a deeper, more intimate connection, bordering on the spiritual. I tried to be passionate but came off clumsy or creepy, and on occasion, both.

I stopped her from walking into the bathroom one night by pinning her against the doorframe because I had seen it in a movie. My fingers snagged her hair, yanked her head backward against the doorframe. She yelped, slapped my chest, and asked what I was doing. I answered, but it sounded like a question, that I was being sexual.

Or the night I rolled over in bed and went to whisper in her ear *Let's bang* but something must have shifted in my body because I choked. I coughed hard into her ear and spit-up Cheez-Its, which, luckily, I caught on my shoulder.

But what really hurt didn't have anything to do with Alice. The truth was I didn't know how to be close to my wife.

For months she talked about sleeping with her ex-boyfriend. It's only sex, she said. I never could argue with her. People were sexual creatures, and if our relationship was strong enough it could survive something merely physical. She said at least she was open about wanting to sleep with someone else, wouldn't things be worse for her to do it behind my back?

You don't own anyone. For men it's ego wedged in the way, I think, and the inability to communicate feelings. My responses would be things like *But we're married* and *If we love each other we should sleep with each other not other people* and *But you're my wife.* And if you think about it, think really hard, those things don't mean a thing. I spoke in clichés and hated myself. I told her to do whatever she wanted because a person could.

After it happened we had a talk where I didn't talk. What could I say? I was mad and frustrated and she wore a black knit top that covered her jeans to her knees. I'm being superficial again. I'm the male gaze again. We tried working through it by attending therapy in a building that also housed a daycare center and a lingerie store. The therapist would ask how I felt and I'd say, "Bad" and she'd urge me to expand on the feeling. I'd stare at the bowl of M&M's on the table until she moved on to Alice. I'd count the few blue ones. Maybe a therapist thing – track what color patients took, which was blue. I wonder what that means.

A few weeks after we stopped going to therapy, Alice and I watched a documentary about the Renaissance. One segment discussed women as the dominant role in the relationship – how the man wasn't important and affairs were accepted because the institution of marriage wasn't widely accepted. Alice said, "Guess I should have lived in those times." I walked into the bathroom, fell to my knees, and punched the carpet around the toilet.

I'm being dramatic again. I'm not being honest. God could slap a lightning bolt through the window and into the cushion next to me but I don't believe in God, maybe something else, a mystery terrifying enough to make me tell the truth. That entails seeing life from Alice's point of view, how she felt in the marriage, trapped with me, how much she had to endure about my retirement, how it's unheard of to leave a State job with the benefits being so good, the glorious payout at the end. I later realized that I only viewed her as parts, not a whole person with agency (thank you, Alice) not a reality severed from my own. She had dreams that didn't include me. When she was offered the national Director's position at RISSE in Chicago I told her I didn't want to move and she replied she already knew that. I figured she wouldn't make such a big move because I wouldn't make such a big move. But she had already made up her mind.

After she left, Elderly said, "What goes around comes around."

"That doesn't make sense," I said.

Some nights I have thoughts of growing really old and owning a cushioned toilet seat, reading glasses on a chain, a metal walker with tennis ball feet, and I'm alone and shuffling to the couch and where is Alice. Is she happy? Yes, she is very happy. Her ideal gate was leaving me.

During the marriage, I found her walking other cities – New York, Los Angeles, Chicago – on Google maps. She wanted a big interesting life and that required a big interesting city. She didn't want a life my parents had already lived. Side-eyed, I watched her lurch forward on pixelated streets.

But are we just going to become wrinkled people living in different cities waiting to die?

Two new emails. One is from my boss, a welcoming kind of thing before tomorrow's first real day back. The second is spam from someone named Crying Sub-God, whose avatar is an anime sumo wrestler with a single white tear stretched and falling to a blue mat. YEAH SHE RIDES HIM is the subject followed by non-sequential numbers and random letters in caps. The internet is a shithole but it's thrilling. I'm disappointed the email isn't about Rudy, who, with the exception of Tom Ruddles, I haven't received one call about.

I get out of bed and pace around my apartment. I do laps. Outside, Elderly is attempting to push the Pontiac from one side of the street – no parking on Tuesdays and Thursdays – to the other side. The temperature has dipped into storm coming weather and he's shirtless, body at a severe angle, head down and shoving the bumper that is ready to fall off, a corner scratching the pavement. It's not exactly allowed by PER to go outside and help, I don't think, but if tomorrow is the first real training day, of being back, I can still function fully in my reality.

"Who is Rudy?"

I don't possess much strength, but somehow we move the Pontiac, crumbling home on wheels, to the opposite side of the street. The back end is easily four feet from the curb. Someone beeps as they pass, and Elderly screams to slow the fuck down. A garbage bag has been torn open by animals and Styrofoam food containers from Chinese restaurants and Dunkin Donuts cover the sidewalk and cling to the hills.

"My dog. My window was smashed out. Remember?" I point to my car across the street, the back window blacked-out in tape I stole from work.

"Nah," says Elderly, out of breath, "but I owe you for dinner. I never forget a favor. I'll get them back for you."

"How's that?"

"Thieves always return to the crime scene. Everyone knows that."

"I don't know that."

"No? In Tehran they came back at night to watch the flames being put out by fire trucks with no water. The Shah had spent a million dollars on a party so they had no budget for emergency services." Elderly pops the hood and studies the corroded parts. I wonder, because he's so talkative, if he's drinking again. Maybe I started something at the diner. Maybe I bought him too much Bud Heavy. "You drive me to the mall three days in a row starting right now and I guarantee they show up," he says, still looking at the engine. "I'll take care of them. Someone who breaks into a car to save a dog, they're looking to do it again. And I don't blame you, the mall is a great place to leave a dog in a car."

"You're in a mood."

"I've found God."

I don't know if he's joking or not.

"You have something else to do? Come on. You're divorced. I could use a drive and so could you. Come on V, come on."

On the drive to the mall we pass under the interstate ramp system, the only one of its kind in America. Before Alice, I commuted thirty minutes in rush hour traffic to campus and when I passed under the five curving ramps ascending fifty yards, maybe more, every inch of every ramp would be bumper-to-bumper with cars. Tonight as we go under the ramps there's hardly anyone at all, only a tractor trailer on the top ramp driving under the moon.

"Trucks carry poison," says Elderly as I take exit five into the mall. "There's very little regulations now. It's how they want it."

"My coworkers eat nothing but Doritos and deli meat."

"It's because they want to die," Elderly says. "Maybe not consciously, but secretively, inside."

Slowly, I drive between the parked cars, many carefully backed in for no reason but to do it. If I'm seen backing into a spot come up from behind in the backseat and slice my throat open. Let my blood spray over the dashboard and onto the windshield. Elderly puts his feet on the glovebox, takes his right shoe off, and inspects a toe. He doesn't smell like alcohol, but grass clippings and sweat. "We're out on the town, V, soaking up American culture. Should we see a movie? Should we buy something at Best Buy?"

The yellow and blue lights of Best Buy are glaring. How do they get so much light in those letters? I drive another loop around the parking lot. Elderly keeps rambling about current events, how he's so aware of them I have no idea. I want to ask why he's so talkative, he hates chit-chat, but it doesn't feel right. I let him talk until he gets it all out.

"Someone burned down the refugee center," I say, then hit the brakes because a white Audi with a license plate HOTSAWCE jolts backward from a front spot. There's no driver in the Audi, or at least it appears so because the interior is all vape clouds. But a head is in there, somewhere. The brake lights combined with my headlights give the clouds a swirling and haunting vibe.

"On a vanity plate you should pay a 300% tax," says Elderly who spits something yellow onto his chin then sucks it up. "Like, that person spent his or her time thinking HOTSAWCE for weeks, maybe years, then went to the DMV and paid a fee, installed it, and now everyone has to see it. How's that fair?"

The car accelerates, the cloud interior flying forward. I follow and turn left. I tell Elderly he's right, it's not fair. A hotel is being built next to the mall and the scaffolding is rung with white lights hung from yellow cables, a coffin-narrow elevator is ascending to the top floor of metal beams.

I drive through another parking lot and down another lane. Elderly says we can go home because he has seen what he needs to see. I don't say a word. He says he misses driving on the highway in his Pontiac, which he insists can still go one hundred miles per hour. He says in the deserts of Iran there's no speed limit, you can drag race any car, and at the finish line children wave checkered flags.

Back on the highway I check the weather on my phone and Elderly, with his big toe, clicks the hazards on.

"Safety first. Finding your dog next." He reclines the seat as far as it will go, his head nearly resting on the back seat.

"I'm sorry, V," he says crossing his arms over his chest and closing his eyes. "But when you're down, you're done."

◎

I'm thinking about the constellation Orion, burning meteorites and Christmas lights. If I had a daughter I'd name her Orion and no one could stop me. I was a child once, and everyone driving to work or taking the bus to work or walking to work was a child once too. I become very childlike before bed, I've always been this way, and it's not embarrassing because who cares, I'm alone.

As a kid, Dad would hang these orange electric candles held by a red plastic wreath in my bedroom window. When I look out my apartment window with the streetlamp outside I can feel my childhood within that light. How does time and space and memory do that? I want to be there, a week before Christmas in the mid 80s because I don't want to be thinking about tomorrow's training.

But I'd be lying if I said I haven't been thinking about what kind of ideal life I'll be living. What will I see? In high school I said I wanted to be a veterinarian because you had to say something. Did you know there are people who drive abused animals around the country finding them homes? The volunteer who inspected my apartment told me it was her dream job, her ideal gate, you could say. She was saving her money for an RV with built-in cages.

I also like the idea of living on a boat, rocked to bed by waves and catching fish at sunrise. I know, that's not me, but…it could be? Or maybe a much simpler life with a house in the country and all the healthy food in the world in surrounding fields and gardens. Is that also not me? My ideal gate could be anything.

A cool night breeze blows under the window. Elderly is lugging a bag of cans down the sidewalk and it sounds like he's running. I'm falling asleep as the gold watch beeps. I flick the tail. Drowsy, I'm ready.

# JUNE 7

In the office I wear my headset and drink my PER water and absolutely demolish data entry. I move numbers from one column to another column then click an icon with the waterfall logo. The headset seems to do nothing but slightly muffle the office around me, which is somewhat helpful – right now Michelle and Steve are discussing Indian food. On occasion, I hear a faint beeping like a train in the distance, which is either the headset, the gold watch, or the train station across the river.

Coming back from the bathroom, I walk by Emily's cubicle and she's inches from her monitor staring at a pixelated horse. She appears on top of the monitor, ready to embrace it. She zooms-in on the horse's left eye, jet-black with a cube of reflected light.

"Great horse," I comment.

"It's Princess," snaps Emily, "and she's mine."

In the Zone, I move onto the next data entry section. There's a consistent flow of new numbers, one column with too many and another column with too few, and the numbers, the task, numb me, like I'm not at a computer but somewhere else, a zone itself that I'm plunging headfirst into.

Still, I don't experience anything different. I'm not seeing any paradise before me. Steve says when you go on vacation in Maine you eat lobster for every meal. He says even if you order pasta you have lobster in every bite.

Francesca forwards an email about a pork chop lunch special.

Michelle forwards a video of her family white water rafting, showing with MS Paint arrows how the three rafts tied together behind them don't contain people, but coolers of Keystone Light.

It's all very depressing, but I don't care because I move the numbers. I submit to PER.

One thing Dorian suggested I do when I arrive to work and when leaving work is close my eyes and count to twenty, then back down to zero, twenty times. Eyes shut, my head feels woozy, like if I stood I'd fall over. Good thing I'm sitting in this chair. I've sat in this chair, minus my stint working from home, for almost ten years. If I complete my training maybe it won't matter so much, but it's possible I'll work until the year 2037 in the same chair.

I complete my first day and begin counting.

Elderly isn't on the street. I notice this much later, after being home and after my routines. His car is here, under the streetlamp, just not him. I check the back seats, then walk around the block, moving through the dark patches of sidewalk between the streetlamps.

Walking in the summer when everyone has their windows open and blinds up is exciting. I love seeing other people's lives. When I was a kid, I wanted to know how everyone else lived. Leaving school for a doctor's appointment and being out in the world with only adults was a new world, but they never seemed to be doing much.

I turn another corner and head back home, peeking into homes, these alive dioramas. In one house, a man is stretching neon colored resistance bands over his head while clenching his teeth and looking in the mirror. In another house, a woman is running up the stairs holding multiple suits with the pant legs dragging on the floor. In another house, the front door is open leading to an all wooden space with a single fluorescent lightbulb. And in the last house before my block, a girl is standing with her arms flat by her sides as her mother does squats.

I eat dinner, do twenty sit-ups, and get into bed at 8 pm exactly, sleeping pills supplied by PER as carnation-pink ovals I roll between my finger and thumb before swallowing. Everything is the same. It's still hot out. I hate sleeping without covers, but the dream is coming.

# JUNE 8

I settle into the Zone and work without a break or speaking a word. Dorian's instructions don't say to avoid my coworkers, but the more I'm achieving my routine the better. Michelle announces from her cubicle that there's pending legislation to change Policeman to Police Officer, and Steve rapid-replies that the world is going to hell in a handbasket. So no ideal gate here, and worst of all, Elderly is gone.

This morning his car had a ticket because it's Thursday, he never moved it, which he never forgets. In all the years I have lived here, Elderly has always been here. He's as much a neighborhood fixture as the trees, the deaf person singing on her way to work, those who walk their dogs daily down the block. He once told me that vehicles appearing to be worth less than five thousand dollars should be exempt from ticketing. I miss him. But if he lived in Iran, and then lived in a car, then maybe he can take care of himself. Maybe he will reappear like nothing ever happened.

Where does a guy like Elderly go? I could file a police report, but it only reminds me of Dad.

I block what I can from my coworkers, adjust the headset, and work diligently with speed. Every minute is a step closer to my ideal gate. Every minute forward is me entering my life. How exciting to be both in control and out of control. On the ride and off the ride. No matter what happens, I have my retirement package waiting for me at the end.

# JUNE 9

I settle into the Zone and work without a break or speaking a word.

# THE WEEKEND

I sleep for 25 hours, and between sleeping, stumble around my apartment.

I'm not depressed. I'm just calm now.

# JUNE 12

I settle into the Zone and work without a break or speaking a word.

# JUNE 13

I settle into the Zone and work without a break or speaking a word.

Blood emails me: "Stunning proficiency."

# JUNE 14

I settle into the Zone and work without a break or speaking a word.

# JUNE 15

I settle into the Zone and work without a break or speaking a word.

# JUNE 16

I settle into the Zone and work without a break or speaking a word.

Blood emails me: "The gate is coming."

# THE WEEKEND

42 hours of sleep.

# JUNE 19

Monday, the last week of training, hooray, zoooom, I see nothing.

Before putting my headphones on Michelle says mandarin oranges make a salad exotic. Steve made popcorn because he needs attention. Emily has begun decorating the office with Fourth of July ribbons and posters.

Any of this could be distracting, but I'm all silence and work, the gold watch blinking with the waterfall logo, which I imagine is Fang Lu and Billy Krol doing their jobs, we're connected I think, but I'm not sure how. I don't ask questions, I just do my job, work toward my ideal gate and the joy I deserve.

There is nothing else to my life but PER, walking to work and home from work, eating, the twenty sit-ups, the pill, and then sleeping. My retirement will be $86,000 annually beginning in 2037, maybe more depending on raises and the completion of the program. It's waiting for me. I can feel it.

I complete work I can't remember a second later, the same motion performed for hours.

For maybe less than an hour everything and everyone around me is temporarily gone, a droning outward as I type. I look only at the screen. Then the office, the cubicle walls, the lights, come back into focus.

# JUNE 20

Walking to work, I pass a gas station with one of the pumps on fire. The transparent orange flames are nearly unnoticeable in the summer light. Maybe what I'm seeing isn't real. Everything else surrounding the pump is untouched and no one seems to notice. A dad is pumping gas with three kids inside his van, each holding a phone. I stare and blink at the perfect dome of flame surrounding the pump. It's real? In the wind I feel increased heat, so I run toward the glass doors advertising purple slushies.

Inside, stationed too close to the door are Bud Light thirty packs displayed in the shape of a car. Where the driver should be is a pool-toy shark with a miniature American flag duct taped to its fin. A banner says to, "Keep it cool with aggressive savings." I look for a worker. Two middle eastern men are behind the counter standing shoulder-to-shoulder, blank faced, staring at me. Behind them are colorful rows of cigarettes and I don't smoke, but I want a pack. It's incredibly clean and air conditioned in here, a cold quiet, the workers still staring as I approach.

I use my professional voice. "One of your pumps, out there," I point behind my shoulder, "it's on fire."

The one on the left sneezes. "We know," he says indifferently. "We're waiting for anyone." He blows his nose into a red and black cloth with stitching as squiggly lines of painted white dots and shrugs.

"It's on fire now," I explain.

"We said *we know*," says the one on the right. "But if we go out there they kill us."

"Who?"

"Jesus, what's wrong with you, man?" says the other, now picking his nose and inspecting his finger between picks. "The people who set the fire." He points out the window with his other hand and toward the flames.

"I don't see anyone," I say, feeling dumb, professional voice defeated. "Wait, who is it? Where?"

A giant man slams two half gallons of butter pecan ice cream down on the counter, forcing me to the side. I say I'm sorry even though there's no reason to apologize. The giant is a hungry mouth breather who asks for a plastic spoon. With black smoke now billowing around the pump I can't see who the clerk is pointing at.

"Are you buying anything," says one of the clerks, the one who sneezed and blew his nose, who is now chewing his fingernails, "or did you just come in here to say we have a fire?"

"Which we already knew about," the other says and spits green gum into his hand. "Which will probably be out from the next storm before anyone helps us. They take their time now. They've picked a side."

"Yeah," says the giant with the butter pecan ice cream, unwrapping the plastic spoon. "Don't you understand what's going on?"

Continuing my walk to work, protesters, scarred-faced men in baggy carpenter jeans and loose fitting leather vests, are holding picket signs telling "All of them" to return home. For someone who works for the State, I don't consider myself a political person, my non-action helps no one, out of all the causes in the world someone would choose a war against an entire religion. What does it matter the land your mother shat you out? Everywhere is everywhere.

When I see protesters like these walking from the gas station I remember what Alice told me. Because it's an easy cause. Anyone can carry a sign that says "My Favorite Color Is Freedom." Anger is lazy. It helps if the anger is fueled by fear and these guys are terrified. They're old enough to have lived through the six o'clock news of the Iran Revolution so they believe it could happen here. But those who run the gas station just want to feed their kids and send them to school with new sneakers and backpacks. Does it work? I don't know. I don't know what I'm talking about. You'd have to ask someone like Alice.

I speed walk to work, excited and ready to enter the Zone.

In the elevator again is Shawl Lady. She wears the shawl tight around her face, red hair visible, very little else besides the green flats. I move to the back corner after hitting the button for my floor, fourteen. Her floor, eighteen, is already lit up.

Elevator silence when it's only a man and a woman present is awkward because the man is usually thinking something sexual about the woman and the woman is thinking she doesn't want to die. Sarah told me that shortly after the stomach touching incident. So I don't say a word to Shawl Lady.

I exit on my floor and turn to look at her. I can't help myself. As the doors close, Shawl Lady is facing the back wall in an oval of black.

# JUNE 21

I settle into the Zone and work without a break or speaking a word.

# JUNE 22

I settle into the Zone and work without a break or speaking a word.

From her cubicle Emily says, "Fuck me, fudge fancies."

Blood emails me: "Last day. Good luck."

# JUNE 23

There's an ongoing conversation about what to order for lunch. It's ten in the morning. Friday in an office environment means Groupon takeout and discussing weekend plans. It doesn't bother me. I do my work and shatter data entry records. I am all go as the office fades in and out. I'm ready to achieve my gate. Even when Steve says that he hates eggs but loves egg foo yung I keep working, clicking the completion tab over and over again.

"Chinese?"

"Brought my lunch."

"Oh, whaja' bring?"

"A sandwich."

"Sounds good."

"We should do Chinese. Jade Palace has a special. General Tso's chicken with fried rice and it comes with those, what do you call them, crab raggins? Whatever those things with the shit inside."

"Raggins."

"Soup please."

"You're doing Groupon, right?"

"Yeah."

"What time should we order?"

"Now."

"Egg roll?"

"I'm in."

"Steve, who are you kidding?"

"Ten for Steve."

"Okay, so I'll put the order in. I figure everyone wants the General Tso's chicken combo with wonton soup?"

"And raggins."

"I want sesame chicken."

"What's the difference?"

"Seeds."

"Yes, hello? Two egg rolls and three General Tso's chicken lunch specials. Sorry, one Sesame chicken. I can't understand a word you're saying. Now that comes with the raggins and wonton soup and fried rice? I want to be sure because last time I didn't get any and I don't want to go through an ordeal again. Still there? Give me the total. I have the Groupon coupon. And when the guy comes have him go to the Edgar street side entrance, thank you."

"Thanks for calling. I hate those people."

"How long?"

"Ugh, didn't say. Hold on."

"Hi. I just ordered, but you didn't tell me how long. Ten minutes? Okay. Thank you."

"They always say ten minutes."

"Was the total like I said?"

"I have an envelope here."

"I'm going to the little girls' room."

"I'm thinking of getting a tattoo on my arm that says Dare To Live."

"I smell popcorn."

"I'm *sooooo* hungry."

"I don't eat breakfast."

"I eat a donut. I know it's bad for me, but sometimes you just have to say hell with it."

"That's why you eat half. Like yesterday, my husband made this egg and cheese sandwich with crispy bacon."

"Wish Todd did that."

"Is someone making popcorn before Chinese?"

"I'm hungry."

"Chalupa?"

"I only ate half because you have to consider calories. Like with this Chinese food, you don't have to eat *all of it*. I save mine for dinner."

"I'll be shocked if it takes ten minutes, absolutely *shocked*."

"Could be one raggin or twenty different things."

"Ten minute."

"Stop it, you're terrible."

"But funny."

"You're not at the Bragg street side are you? It's a real pain to get, hahaha, okay, good. We'll be right down. Hey Steve, you mind going down to get the food, my feet hurt."

"Your feet always hurt when you have to do something."

"Or when she's hungover."

"Which is always."

I'm walking home with a headache. My personal record for this walk is thirty five minutes and I'm going to break it in twenty three, occasionally jogging, speed walking when I can't jog. In my life I set records.

At a stop light, the driver in a jeep, college aged in an orange tank top and desert storm shorts, who has hit every red light on my path so far, tells me to slow down. But I can't slow down because I've completed my training, so I wave and say, "I can't slow down!"

then turn down my block and into the evening sunshine filtered through the trees.

Everything is exactly the same – the squirrels darting across the street, the stench of heated garbage waiting to be picked up, those without AC sitting on their porches, joggers in yoga pants, dogs shitting, the flowers, the bikes, the cars. The only change is the disappearance of Elderly, who I fear the worst given his age, mental state, and lifestyle – living shirtless in a 1995 Pontiac Bonneville.

I'm a dope, walking up the concrete steps to my apartment believing the program could really show me something else, but this is what the State does. They pay exorbitant fees to tech companies who dazzle with presentations given by men in skinny ties and degrees from Ivy league schools. By men named Dorian Blood, Fang Lu, and Billy Krol. The State has no idea what these companies actually do, but they're seduced by the technology, the colored charts, the dimming lights in the conference room signaling a big budget presentation.

The Leaders want nothing to do with technology themselves. When a firm in 2005 supplied iPhones and a new web system for each Leader none of them participated, because they had to physically do it. But when Cordo & Co. came in with monitoring devices because so many employees weren't showing up to work, they were for it, they didn't have to run the devices. Because they don't care how diabolical or bizarre these programs are as long as money is saved, productivity goes up, and they don't have to finger a screen.

I drop my keys at the front door – on a mat supplied by my landlord that reads CHRIST IS THE HEAD OF THE HOUSE – and think how boring. My life. My life is boring. In the mailbox I have three pieces of mail from three different banks, a sushi coupon, and a flyer advertising Fourth of July fireworks.

Someone inside my apartment is talking.

I close the door, making sure not to make a sound.

Now I don't hear anything. I think about knocking on my own front door knowing it's impossible that someone could be in there who isn't me. When I place my keys back in my pocket I touch two pills. My landlord didn't say anything about the plumber, or a worker stopping by, I don't think. Through the past days of PER training, I can't remember.

I run from the porch and to the side of the house, bending down low between the side and bathroom windows.

Crouching below my bedroom window, my heart is racing in that way where you think you're going to have a heart attack, but you never actually have the heart attack. The human body is powerful when it comes to stress response. It can absorb great storms. I can't hear anything inside my apartment, but my next door neighbor has purchased an acoustic guitar. He wants to play so his windows are open. I don't know much about my neighbor besides his children are always shirtless.

I get the courage to stand, peek into the window, and sitting on my bed is a woman with just her back visible, maybe Shawl Lady, I can't tell.

I should call the police. A stranger in my apartment is a crime. I could call my landlord, but he hates me because the sink broke and he said it was my fault for rinsing coffee grinds down the drain. He said the damage was identical to my security deposit. When it comes to money, humanity goes out the window.

All around me is the summer buzzing of bugs, kids screaming in pools, bass from cars, and my neighbor strumming his new guitar.

I peer into the window again. This time I take a long look so what I'm seeing feels real. There's definitely a person in there, but it's not Shawl Lady, it's Alice.

Frantically trying to remember the rules of interacting with my gate I go dizzy. I crouch back down and take a few deep breaths. My neighbor stops playing guitar and from his window asks if everything is okay and I say everything is amazing.

"Amazing?"

"Yeah," I say. "Amazing."

I'm walking into my apartment. I can do this. My new mantra: I will live in my gate and be happy.

But now there's no voice coming from the bedroom, only water running in the kitchen. Dramatically, I toss my keys on the table with the TV, a move I never do, hoping the sound will alarm whoever (Alice, I love you) might still be here. I walk toward the kitchen, more thief than resident in my own home.

The hallway takes forever to navigate. All the windows in my apartment are open except the forever-stuck front one, I can tell, because my neighbor is now playing Dave Matthews, I think, he can't sing in the slightest, but the lyrics are familiar. In my final step before the kitchen I take one long and slow stride.

I am terrified.

Now I'm at the spot where the hardwood floor becomes these junky press-and-seal faux kitchen tiles the landlord hasn't replaced since I moved in, most of them peeling at the corners. Alice is washing her hands in the sink. On the stove is a boiling pot of water. My face must look ridiculous in its total shock. I'm not breathing, I'm panting. Above the sink the lilac tree is swaying violently in the beginning winds of another storm.

I don't say a word and she doesn't notice me.

She's wearing baggy black sweatpants with a long drawstring hanging between her legs and a black spaghetti string top with three tiny holes. Her rarely washed curly hair is in a rubber band ponytail. All very Alice. It smells like her, a mix of Nag Champa and sweat. Even her shoulder tattoo – a solid black circle with curved Arabic lettering outside of it – is here.

I step forward and into my gate.

I fake cough against my trembling fist.

She turns and says, "Hey you, the cheese?"

I'm stunned and sweating and Dave Matthews is playing. My first eye contact with Alice. She still has the same power over me, she consumes me, drains me. If that sounds odd, it's not, every relationship has a stronger one. I would do anything for her and she knows it.

I run my hands down my face and she's still here. I gather myself and pull the professional me above and out my constricted throat, asking, "The cheese?"

"For the pasta," she says, dumbfounded. "I told you this morning before work? And texted you?"

I pull my phone from my pocket and there it is, a one word text from a number I don't recognize – CHEESE – followed by three thick red hearts.

"Oh yeah," I reply, "you did."

Every day since Alice left and the podium incident and working from home and PER training becomes compacted into a single moment, a thought cloud, *poof*.

"See a doctor," says Alice.

I don't question this version of Alice or attempt to touch her while entering my gate. There are more rules. I need to grab my list. Let the gate guide me is one, so go get the cheese, you jabroni. Still, I stand in the kitchen just staring. Everything else appears the same, my reality is still my reality. No beach front property or champagne colored Lexus or in-ground swimming pool or Tudor-style home with five bathrooms, only Alice. It's perfect.

I mumble the word cheese and smile.

"What's wrong with you?"

"Nothing."

"Nothing?"

"Yeah, nothing."

She slumps her shoulders and walks across the kitchen, away from the coming storm now slapping the lilac tree from side-to-side. Here comes Alice, across two hundred days until her body is pressed against mine.

"Sorry for being mean," she mumbles. "Just had a rough day. Love you."

"I love you too." My brain is boiling and my legs are liquid. I put my arms around her and my hands don't move through her.

I walk in a near run to the grocery store. I pass RISSE, which is now being rebuilt with yellow and green signage. A landscaper waves hello with a leaf blower strapped to his back, a handful of grass blows into the sky. Everything is brighter now. Boys in black thobes and girls in pastel hijabs are playing soccer to the far side of the building as a teacher shouts for them to come inside.

A man in a shirt, BEASTMODE, is vaping at the grocery store entrance, exhaling with his head tilted back. I pass through all clouds and into the store. My future is here and it's Alice.

In the dairy section a woman is holding thirty yogurts. She's balancing them by leaning the containers against her leaning back body and walking backward. Surprisingly, it's working, she only drops one from her right shoulder, which someone scoops up and places right back on her. I pull the folded paper of PER rules, taken from the bedroom before leaving, from my pocket:

1. Do not confront the gate about its plausibility.
2. Do not question humans inside the gate.
3. Do not control the gate.
4. Let the gate guide you.
5. Do not attempt to escape the gate.
6. Documenting the gate by video or photo is prohibited.

But is Alice in my apartment an image of Alice or a clone or… Should have paid closer attention to the training video. I think this guy behind me is going to steal some frozen shrimp. What cheese do I buy so Alice doesn't leave me again? My head is blurry. The arrival of Alice brings on a new level of anxiety, like everyone can see my thoughts. I want to talk to Elderly. One person leaves, another comes back. Can I kiss her? Can I bring her outside? Can others see her? Accept your life while standing in the dairy section of the grocery store. Guy behind me is loading up two reusable bags with frozen shrimp, good for him, he needs it more than anyone else in here. I grab the cheese.

Back home, I'm so on edge I sit at the table with extreme uncomfortable posture. She asks if everything is okay, and I say yes, everything is fine, why, the cheese? It is definitely the wrong kind, but she's being pleasant so she doesn't say a word. I can't stop staring. I want to touch her again even though I know it's prohibited (let the gate guide you, right). I'm trying to act like all this is normal.

"Okay, let's start over. How was work?" she asks. "Francesca still pissed?"

I struggle to speak, but what comes out is natural and resembles us from years ago. "Steve said he likes egg foo yung in a Chinese voice," I say, relaxing a little.

"Oh my God," laughs Alice, sprinkling cheese onto her pasta, her favorite meal. She eats pasta constantly, making a large pot and stretching it out over the course of the week in multiple Tupperware dishes.

"Then they ordered Chinese food," I add.

"I don't know how you work there," she says, shaking her head. "RISSE clients survived a civil war, and you have people there mocking foreign voices, people who sit in an office with no threats and a big retirement. It's unbelievable."

"I did this online calculator thing," I say spinning spaghetti on my fork, "where I can retire in twenty years. I'm close to ten. It doesn't seem so bad, but just saying the date 2037 sounds fake."

"Most of your life," she points out correctly. "What happens if you don't make it to ten?"

"I lose everything I put in."

"But you still get a small piece?"

"Nope."

"That's fucked up."

"Michelle told us that a pig can have an orgasm for thirty minutes."

Again, I stare. She's real.


"Let's do something tomorrow. It's boring just sitting around the apartment all weekend. Maybe the castle? It's been awhile. What do you think?"

I feel both scared and excited. "Sure."

With her fork she acknowledges my plate. "Not eating?"

"At work Sarah brought in bagels and I ate three."

Alice shrugs and I spend the rest of the meal watching her and feeling hungry.

"This guy at the store was stealing bags of frozen shrimp," I say.

"That's perfect," says Alice. "He needs it more than us."

Alice walking to the bedroom (Please don't disappear in there).

Alice sitting on the couch reaching for the remote (I'll watch something with you).

Alice rubbing lotion on her legs (Want me to do it?).

Alice sipping seltzer (Where does it go?).

Alice breathing (Do you have the same heart?).

I pretend I need to use the bathroom as she is leaving the bathroom. I slightly bump into her because I need to know she is authentic, which, shoulder-to-shoulder, she is. "Watch it," she says.

Together we open the windows because we want to feel the cool air following a storm, and someone from a passing car yells that they have "big booty bitches." In a conference-call voice Alice replies, "Congratulations."

11:45 pm

Alice is sleeping so I carefully slide in next to her. Something falls on my leg, I panic, it's a phone, but no, it's her hand. I move to the edge of the bed and her hand falls further, her fingers grazing my leg. I'm so excited I nearly laugh. In my delirium, I place my hand over my face like a spider and squeeze hard enough to distract myself from the fact that Alice is here.

1:37 am

She sweats like a child – droplets cover her nose – when she dreams.

3:45 am

I place one fingertip on her chest and remove it like touching a hot stove when her heart beats.

5:47 am

Her leg now over my body, mouth parted, the daylight opening the bedroom. I am so exhausted. I imagine Alice disintegrating in the sunshine soon-to-be at our ankles. Hope for clouds. What will happen to her when we're at the castle?

5:49 am

The castle is a one hour train ride south located on a hill, miles of surrounding farmland with flower-bordered paths and radiant lakes, previously owned in the 1850s by Frederic Church. A tourist destination for those too afraid to go on a real vacation. People like it because it's a castle. Young artists visit for inspiration because Church said the property was an attempt to create a holistic and heavenly environment for creativity. It's like going back in time, nothing has changed from when Church lived there with his wife. You can even walk into the area of the house where the help lived, which is a half room with no electricity and dresser drawers for beds. I'm never sleeping.

6:30 am

Trying now, but at this point, it's a nap. Where's the cut-off? Alice sleeps through the garbage truck rumbling down the street, the plastic bins thrown across the sidewalk, the deaf person singing, my whistling nose, the world.

# THE WEEKEND

I'm buying coffee and croissants, standing near the expanding line waiting to board the train. Once Alice is confronted with the cashier's eye-contact she will vanish, portal-like, I am sure of it. But she just looks down when I'm handed my coffee and croissant. Alice says she isn't hungry. The ideal gate is real, and Dorian's philosophy of the fantasy acting as a transparent-covering on my reality holds true. What if we had a baby? The line is moving.

We're heading to the castle, the river passing by smooth as glass. The guy in front of us is playing a machine-gun video game with the sound loud because he thinks his headphones are plugged in. Doesn't matter, all I can concentrate on is my leg touching Alice's leg. It could be seconds or minutes, who knows, where I'm moving my thigh back-and-forth, not connecting with her, then connecting with her.

"Are you okay?" she asks, moving her leg from mine. "Too much coffee?"

"I'm good."

She shifts over in her seat. "When you drink too much coffee you're weird."

"Not too much coffee," I say holding a coffee, "just didn't sleep much."

"So?" Her demeanor changes. "Does that give you the right to put your body on my body?"

What year Alice is this? What I mean – is this her at the beginning of our relationship, how it felt last night when she appeared, or is this Alice toward the end, which, based on what she just said to me is here now. She puts her hand on my leg and turns to the side in her seat, facing me. Through the window a motorboat is spraying a wake and struggling to keep up with the train. It's not a race but it feels like one. Boats aren't faster than trains. The guy playing the video game is using a flamethrower now. "Don't shut down, be present with me," says Alice. "You need to be aware."

"You always say that. I know what you mean, but also, I don't. How can I be talking to you right now and not be here?"

"I know what you mean," she mimics slack-jawed, "but also, I don't."

*Do not control the gate.*

Okay.

*Let the gate guide you.*

Yes.

We're walking the winding path toward the castle. Some people ride the shuttle because they like to sit as much as possible. The man playing the video game is still playing, headphones now plugged in. His body is small and kind of twisted up. He's with his mother and they're driven in a separate shuttle, a camouflage golf cart with chrome rims, careening up the hill.

"Do you ever think of painting again?" she asks as we ascend the thick gravel path. An older couple to the side of us is really struggling. They move as if walking through a pool of oil. Then the man throws his hands up and heads carefully back down the hill, arms extended like he's touching walls, saying, "I can't do this anymore...*with you.*"

Maybe those who like to sit have the right idea.

"Not really," I say shrugging. "I'm not sure I was ever good at it. I'm okay with it."

"You sap."

"It's true," I say, letting her shove me. "I'm happy at my day job and living with you. I don't need much."

"Holy shit this place is making you sentimental. What happened?"

"Nothing. What happened to you?"

She stops abruptly and I think maybe she'll disappear, that I've accidently challenged the gate. But her stopping is her way to convey shock at me implying something *had* happened to her. I apologize. I don't do a thing to mess my gate up, no way, uh-uh. She starts walking again.

Inside the castle we escape the tour. Holding hands, we walk the narrow staircases. When Church designed the interior he hand-painted and stenciled everything in middle east décor, Persian style, the pamphlet said, so there's lots of brushed gold and faded emerald. Yellow poppies decorate doorways. The money flowing into this place – the admission and parking fee, the gift shop – goes to the State. Historical preservation is the explanation, but it's just straight cash flowing into the "General fund" which my office uses to print signs and banners for one time use.

On the top floor, Alice steps over a thick rope leading to Church's bedroom. She stands on a rug weaved in blood-orange and elephant hide colors. "Don't do it," I whisper.

"Come on," she replies. "Who cares?"

Alice has always been into adventure. During one of our first dates she jumped the bar to pour a drink because the bartender was in the bathroom taking a shit. She served beers on tap to strangers and accepted tips. Early Alice caused spontaneous scenes, later Alice drank half-beers and became so fearful she couldn't drive more than forty miles per hour. I don't blame her, it's one of my holes too, driving on a highway is taking a chance on a metal coffin, it's why we took the train to the castle.

"No way," I say to Alice tip-toeing around Church's bedroom.

"Get in here," she whispers.

Walking away would equal escaping the gate, so I follow into Church's ornate bedroom that minus cleaning staff probably hasn't had two people in it for a hundred plus years.

"We're going to get arrested," I tell Alice.

"Just two minutes," she says.

For a guy who was into painting landscapes he sure liked peacocks. They are everywhere. As painted statues six feet tall, framed illustrations hung on the walls, and stenciled on each tile leading into bathroom. Church's bed, which Alice swan dives onto, is domed by peacock colored netting. The windows are amber colored and honeycombed with black lines. How all of this was not burned to the ground by the workers in the back quarters, I don't know.

She swings her legs off the side of the bed and inspects a brass bowl on a wooden nightstand. Every piece of furniture has knotted lace-like carvings running the edges, more peacock paintings on the front and sides, dog-pawed feet. Nothing is simple here. Even the lamp on the dresser appears to be constructed from ten different parts, more flower than utility piece. Alice walks to the dresser and begins opening every drawer. They have gold hinges shaped like dragonflies with red screws for eyes. Most are empty except random papers and cleaning supplies, but inside one drawer is a notebook, leather-bound and badly worn.

"Open it," says Alice, who tries handing me the book by waving it near my face.

"You open it."

"Ugh," she grunts. "Fine."

I step closer. "But I want to see."

"Who wouldn't?"

Inside are women's names and their daily tasks to complete inside and outside the home, written by Church himself, his initials on each corner, his handwriting a flowing but severely slanted longhand, two columns of names and tasks separated by a black line. I turn the pages with endless names. In the final pages are the household rules. Alice points to a single sentence on a page otherwise blank: "Clean all horse stalls of all blood."

The bathroom is wallpapered with wreaths of cherries against a desert dune background. Alice steps into the bathtub with a peacock faucet. She lays with her arms crossed over her chest, eyes closed. There are no windows in here. I look in the bathroom mirror above the sink and flick my nose.

"Were you ever inspired by this place?" she asks, sitting up in the tub. "Did you really sit on the lawn and paint the river?"

"I did," I confess. "You really shouldn't be in there."

I panic because what I just said could be challenging my gate. But Alice nods. She doesn't disappear. I stare, breathing deeply, convinced that at any minute we will be caught and charged with numerous trespassing accusations, then I'll be fired from my job. I was so close to the ten year mark.

"You're right," she says, now standing. She straddles the side of the tub, carefully steps out, then sits on the toilet.

Do whatever you want.

I won't stop you, Alice.

Let Alice be Alice.

"Don't tell Mr. Church," she says, shifting her pants down to her knees. The sound of piss on porcelain is incredibly loud.

Early years Alice forever.

Leaving the bedroom, she takes a silver paintbrush from the windowsill vase and slips it inside the waist of her jeans, and when I glare in judgement, in amazement, she shrugs.

As the tour continues up the stairs, we walk down the back stairs to the dining hall, a massive room with no windows and a cement colored banquet table set ornately for fifty. The main vibe in the castle is Church and his wife were lonely, constantly adding décor to the walls, fixtures and trinkets to whatever space, no matter how small, not yet touched. A crowded atmosphere – I overhear the tour guide say "Artful clutter" – with little natural light.

We walk through the dining hall. Alice checks the hallway for anyone, and when it's clear, we go further down into what is the basement.

Even here everything is ornately decorated, but this is a different style room, renovated and added recently to display the worker's portraits, the names from the book. It's an afterthought, a pandering political move by Leader Dubben (first name Reuben, which is the best rhyming name ever) representing the district, and it's the saddest of the rooms. Because Church didn't design it, it feels out of place. One picture shows a woman frowning next to the horse stalls.

"Unbelievable," says Alice, touching everything she can, running her hand over the portraits, stepping over the roped off areas with more furniture and arranged vases. She sits down in a queen-like chair. "I love you," she says.

There's an hour before the train leaves so we're at the lake, sitting on the sand with our knees pulled to our chests, me lovingly mocking how Alice is sitting. She rests her head against my shoulder. The world is silent and the wind white-tops the waves. It's much cooler here because of the elevation, I think, a hint of fall in summer or another storm coming, but the cloudless sky is aggressively blue.

The lake Church painted and made a fortune off glimmers like a metal roof. That lake deserves to be paid. You can rent a rowboat for two dollars but we won't. The man playing the violent video game is out there, his mother struggling to row in the wind.

I put my arm around Alice and my arm doesn't pass through her.

I put my mouth on her head.

Shifting backward, she comes to a kneeling position. Above her is the castle and the white outline of the moon. A mist of sand blows through the air and into us and her hair wraps around her face. She asks if I just kissed her.

I'm enamored with all things Alice, this very real version I want to consistently touch confirming this is happening. I need to ask Dorian how long the gate will last. Does it close-up or stay this way forever? I didn't think a person could be the focal point of an ideal gate. Will I be retired with Alice? And if I go first will she have access to my pension? I know the answer to the last question – it's yes, because she's listed as the beneficiary. In the future my retirement transfers to Alice so she can have a comfortable life after I'm dead.

"You did this." She palms my head and pushes it downward. "Like, you put your mouth on my head," she mumbles into my hair, "but you didn't actually do a kiss." I'm looking into the sand. Everything is slightly darker in here. Alice presses her lips hard against my hair for a dramatically long time making a sucking noise then kneels backward again.

"Thank you," I say to the sand.

◉

On the train ride back she falls asleep with her head on my lap. She drools. The guy still playing the violent video game is across the aisle from me, also in the aisle seat, and asks if – he points at Alice – is a video game. His chin is touching his chest but his eyes are fixated on me.

"It's my wife," I whisper. "It's a person."

"But."

"My wife," I say, leaning over slightly so he can hear me.

"But."

"*Shhhhhhhh* she's sleeping."

"But."

The man twitches and his legs that don't reach the floor spasm. His head moves in a circle. "But," he says, "But but but," louder and louder until people are turning around, until his mother is glaring at me from the window seat, cradling his vibrating head in a soothing rocking motion. With my hands cupping her ears, Alice doesn't move.

I decide to no longer be a people watcher.

The train rocks along toward A-ville as Alice sleeps. Two teenage girls keep going to the bathroom and each time they come out they have more make-up on. Some people have laptops open, there's a woman sitting two rows up with some kind of wrap or shawl around her head, typing away. I'm not sure these people are interesting, but I can't stop being a people watcher. A small man in a big suit is watching *Pineapple Express* but isn't laughing. Most sleep on the train like Alice, heads wobbling against the seat or window. I think these people are fake sleeping. I won't wake Alice until the train conductor tells me it is time to go. The sky is getting dark.

Driving home from the train station she asks what happened to the back window. I tell her I bought a dog named Rudy who was sick, who I left in the car, and someone broke the window because they thought he was too hot. Alice doesn't take her eyes off me. I tell her Rudy is dead, if he wasn't given medication. I describe his blood-tongue, greasy fur, and how he ran at the park, so thrilled. I tell her about the vet. She sits sideways in the passenger seat but doesn't respond. She's just looking at me, her blank expression never changes, she doesn't find the vet funny at all. With her window down we drive in the rain and she doesn't say a word about getting wet, an entire side of her body becoming soaked.

Alice has strict rituals around bedtime. Now that she's back, I'm sure not to disrupt them.

What I would do – flossing my teeth while walking into every room, breathing too loud, eating cereal while standing in the living room, entering a room only to ask what she's doing – are details she had mentioned to the therapist. But now I give her plenty of space, admiring her from a distance as she: makes tea, slices an apple on a cutting board, blows out the candle in the bathroom, grinds coffee for the morning, folds the sheets down on our bed with the headboard she has recently strung with white lights.

Next to her, I can't sleep. I don't want time to move forward. Everything is thrown into the past too quickly. The castle is already gone. And if this Alice is somewhere in the middle of our marriage, she only has one place to go. I want my gate tomorrow to repeat today. I need everything to slow down.

Years ago I was really into reading about black holes. I had learned everything I could about stars. I found a video online where a professor at MIT said that any object approaching a black hole slows down, and once inside, freezes. So hypothetically speaking, Alice could walk into a black hole to preserve herself. But from her perspective, if she stood waving from inside the black hole for me to enter and be with her, I would be speeding up. She'd see me accelerating into the future, stars smeared to the sides as she remained in a forever second. So for us to stop the gate we would need to walk together, hand-in-hand, leg-to-leg, hip-to-hip, into the black hole.

# JUNE 26

Someone is knocking on my door with their fist. The reason why I can't hear my doorbell is because the doorbell is too loud, an old firehouse design in the kitchen that I have dulled by wadding-up a paper towel and jamming it between the little metal arm and the little metal bell. If you walk directly beneath it you can hear a slight buzzing sound like bees trapped in a glass.

People like to lock their doors, they value their space and silence, and doorbells they love. In ten years I've probably locked my door twice. Same with my car. One time I found Elderly sleeping across the back seat and when I touched his shoulder he was still dreaming. He slapped my hand away and said to hold his goblet of fire.

I kiss sleeping Alice on her forehead, put my sweatpants on, and walk through my apartment, the knocking continuing.

At the door is a man with a blonde brush cut, muscular build, and a white polo shirt tucked into pleated khakis. On his hip hanging from a thin black belt is a gun. After I say hello he opens a manila folder. It's cool out, low-level fog clinging to the street, but quickly burning off with the coming heat.

Cops make some people nervous, but not me. Dad was a cop so I know how to talk to them. I'm not sure why he became a cop besides there wasn't anything else to do. The pay and retirement were good, but his personality didn't fit the role. Be a big phony with small talk and cops are on your side. This one just stands here, shaven face all sweaty, gazing into the folder like an abyss.

"Can I help you, officer?" I ask thoughtfully.

Racing down the street on bikes come boys in white thobes and blue prayer caps. Because my street declines, they coast. One is shirtless and riding with no hands, leaning back, his arms stretched outward with his bike invisible in the fog.

Clearing his throat, the cop introduces himself as Sergeant Bell. He's probably here because of Dorian, an obvious illegal activity the State has been irresponsible enough to support, but I'm wrong, because what he does next is hold up a photo of Elderly. It's from fifteen or twenty years ago, maybe from his Tehran days.

"Yes," I say, even though I'm not asked a question. "That's him."

After Elderly's car was towed and never claimed at the garage a missing person claim was filed. Bell talks cop style – with force and no eye contact. My name was written in a journal, in the car's user manual, and on napkins, all in the glove box along with two thousand dollars.

I say, "That's a lot of money for a guy who lives in his car."

Bell acts surprised. He says Elderly owns four homes. One, says Bell, has no electricity, the copper wires have been stripped from the walls. Another is infested with mice and teenage squatters. The exception is where his wife lives. He points up the street as I look like I'm part of a massive practical joke. He says they don't have much of a relationship, she doesn't even seem too concerned about his recent disappearance, although she did file the missing person claim. "You didn't know any of this?"

"No."

If learning this isn't surprising enough, two of the homes are on my block, slightly down and across the street. The same homes he would weedwack and then go sleep in his Pontiac parked directly in front. Why he never tried to live in the homes, fix them up, Bell says is above his paygrade, a saying often repeated by my coworkers whenever they are asked to work. I can't imagine owning one home. No house left behind where strangers can walk through pointing at furniture they want for a cheap price, trying on my shoes and dress shirts.

Bell says to contact me if I hear anything regarding Elderly's whereabouts, flipping me his business card between his fingertips. The back of the card is autographed with a smiley face in the bottom right corner and has a greasy sheen. A cell phone number is handwritten above the station number.

"I will," I lie.

I watch Bell from my windows. After knocking on my neighbor's door, who doesn't answer, he drives away in a white Dodge Charger, turning his sirens on to pass through a red light at the end of the block.

I'm still in sweatpants and a white t-shirt with yellow pit stains, but I do a quick walk around the block for Elderly, wondering where his wife lives, and if she too has ever lived in a car. I move quickly. Besides a rotting raccoon on the sidewalk no one is around; it's already too hot out. I need to be inside with Alice.

Alice is on the couch reading a book so I'm going to ask her to be Leg Wobble Man with me. If I can get her on my side forever, she has to be Leg Wobble Man with me now. Early year's Alice would do it, but divorcer Alice will refuse.

I'm standing in the room like an idiot, trying to find the right approach and failing. Coming into the apartment every time and seeing her is shocking. But before I ask her, on TV, which she has muted, the local news shows a collaged photo of men who appreciate the Neo-Nazi look – shaved head, blotchy, ugly, white t-shirt – with a list of charges pertaining to the gas station arson. For such an important development it's a quick story, seconds long before a slanted caption – FOURTH OF JULY FAMILY FUN SPECTACULAR – spins on the screen followed by an ad for mouthwash with a girl spooning a frog into her mouth.

"They won't serve a day in jail," says Alice, book raised in front of her face. "Boner is the judge."

I tell her I was there. The book drops an inch.

"When it was on fire?"

"Yeah, I walked in and told them."

"But you didn't do anything?"

"I didn't do anything to a fire?"

Asking her to be Leg Wobble Man is risky, but if this is my ideal gate then we will be Leg Wobble Man together. Love is two people sharing the burden of living and refusing to give up with joyful moments of insanity. The end of love is when each person is consistently asking what the other person is doing, what they are thinking, why did they say what they said or why aren't they talking *enough*.

I ask her to be Leg Wobble Man with me.

"Walk to the kitchen first," she says, scheming behind the book. "Then come back and you'll know my decision."

"What's in the kitchen?"

The news is now advertising fireworks on the plaza. It shows the event from previous years. A man with a boa constrictor around his shoulders is walking through a crowd of people holding star-shaped balloons. Red text slants across the corners of the screen. Children under six months are free and adults can enter a hotdog eating contest. Steve is in the background drinking a beer.

"Go find out," says Alice.

"You'll be here when I get back?"

"Maybe."

"Are you going to be Leg Wobble Man with me or not?"

"Maybe."

The hallway feels like a tunnel. Everything feels slower. The last time I asked her to be Leg Wobble Man she said she couldn't believe this was her life and collapsed despondent on the couch where Alice is right now.

You shouldn't touch a crying person unless you have the magic. Elderly told me that. He said to either be really close or really far away, no in between, no standing a few feet away looking dumb. Because I was outside with Elderly I was far away, but it still felt awful with Alice up there ready to leave me.

I run a few steps, then jump into the kitchen before turning around and walking back to where Alice is, crouched low and shaking her legs.

"I'm so fast," she says, biting her bottom lip.

"Not bad," I say impressed and ready to wobble, "but check me out."

We shake like our knees will hit and bruise but they never will. We laugh like maniacs. There is no pain here. We can't hurt because we are Leg Wobble Man and we're in love.

Alice watches me leave for work. She sits waving at me from the top concrete step. I am happy and also not. For every interaction with Alice there's a secondary thought that this isn't real, my mind correcting then erasing then correcting again, jumping from PER life to real life.

Near the end of the block I turn around and she's Leg Wobble Man. I don't like admitting this, I don't speak in these terms, but I feel, in the moment, blessed. Not by God or a spell, but by the person who has altered what I see. Dorian Blood has changed my life.

◉

At work I try to take the elevator to floor twenty but the button won't light-up. A man delivering a pizza is with me. He's around seventy years old, wearing a sweatshirt with a pattern of the cosmos and a red hat with a trident logo. His hands tremble. I hit the button for floor twenty again.

I know I'm not supposed to go to floor twenty after my gate appeared, but I want to ask Dorian if this is it, Alice in my life again, and I'm not missing something.

What makes my gate so unusual, compared to the testimonials in the video and information in the packet, is there's no material consumption. There's no object, there's no new home or exotic landscape with expanding roses. My physical reality is still strong – on my walk to work today I passed elaborate graffiti on a brick wall that just said HAM. After thumb-pressing floor twenty again I hit the button for fourteen, which is already lit up.

"This for you? Pizza in the morning? Don't get too many but becoming more common, yeah, pizza for breakfast, the way things are, why not." The pizza man shakes his head in disbelief.

"Must be for my coworkers," I say. "They don't care what time it is."

"That's funny," he says without smiling. "I worked with a guy who always ate lunch at noon exactly. Didn't matter if he was hungry or not, had to have lunch not a minute sooner or later. Saw that guy in the bathroom all the time. Huh. Come to think of it, if he was always in the bathroom, means I was always in the bathroom."

I ask how much for the pizza.

Since the cupcake incident and the training I haven't really been part of the office. I want to perform an act of kindness so I feel less guilty, which never works, but I'm going to try anyways. Buying pizza will impress my coworkers and show that I care about them with money and I'm going to make it a big production. In the rising elevator I feel transcendent.

"But never sold pizza in an elevator before," says the pizza man counting a wad of bills taken from his money clip. "Once sold a sausage pizza to a priest in a hardware store. I think that's the weirdest one. Yeah, definitely the weirdest. I didn't even ask what he was doing there, why he was waiting in the hardware store. He wasn't buying anything."

"Except a pizza," I say.

"Hey, that's true."

Saturn is on his sweatshirt where his heart is, surrounded by yellow rings, and further out, suspended stardust. The patches of space around his shoulders are black holes. I ask where he bought such a sweatshirt, one I could never wear, and he says Walmart, fourteen bucks, they have them in a crate near the hunting section.

Victorious, I place the boxes on the snack table next to Emily's cubicle and begin opening the cardboard tops, displaying pizzas in beautiful ways. From the center of the room I shout, "Pizza party!"

Cheese, pepperoni, mushroom, wafting through the office before 9, this is the fucking life. Steve is on the phone, whispering, and Emily comes over and looks at the pizza like she's never seen pizza before. Michelle is in Sarah's cubicle saying she has mini Vodkas stashed in her filing cabinet. The air conditioning kicks on in a whirl. Next to where I'm standing the fax machine grinds out an $89 Cancun vacation, and because no one but Emily is ready to eat I know I've done something wrong.

"Thanks for this," she says, slowly taking a paper plate.

I grab the Cancun ad, pretend to be interested, then place it back on the Xerox. I just stand in the office, doing nothing, feeling guilty, watching the Xerox screen blink from white to green.

"Look," says Francesca, grabbing me by the upper arm and pulling me from the room. She walks hunched over and shuffles her feet like a dachshund. I had no idea she even walked into the room. Her foot speed is a superpower silent glide over office carpeting.

She brings me into the conference room which is decorated in rainbow streamers, rainbow banners, and a rainbow sign most likely printed by Steve – HAPPY ENGAGEMENT EMILY – with a running border of purple horses. Francesca says the surprise party is now ruined, swiping her hands in a downward and outward fashion symbolizing the flattening of earth.

Walking to the Zone, everyone is eating, alone, in their cubicle. They know I've been scolded so it's okay to eat. I use paper towels (people love them) to clean the Zone, everything covered in lunch-dust because I'm disgusting and haven't cleaned since the fifteen day training ended last Friday, that two week fog I can't quite remember.

I want to tell Michelle and Steve and Emily and Sarah that Alice is back, but it's against the rules. Those who saw life as driving a boat while draped in jewelry or owning unbelievable amounts of square footage, wide lawns of fresh sod, didn't tell anyone close to them, so I won't say anything either. Besides, they haven't gotten over the cupcake incident, and now I've ruined Emily's surprise party. I will never be forgiven. I settle into the Zone and work without a break or speaking a word.

◎

I eat a slice of room temperature pepperoni pizza and predict a stomach ache. My work output is like no other, and when I think about Alice back home my thoughts beam. I become filled with the energy I had when we first met.

My boss says floor twenty is closed for cleaning. I don't believe him, it just feels like he's lying, because some people when they lie their voice changes. When my boss lies he gets high-pitched like Mickey Mouse. But I say okay, pretending to believe him.

Back in the Zone I finish my work and begin counting.

I walk home in a near run to see Alice. It's so hot that in the distance everything including the air is wavy, and what I see, what it looks like on the sidewalk blocks away are four people holding crowbars, dancing over a body.

As I walk closer, they throw their weapons at passing cars, shattering windshields, the cars driving outward to the sidewalks. Before I get too close, I turn onto the next block. But music is playing from where I just walked, a crashed radio, and I can't un-see what I think I just saw. Sometimes reality is too difficult for one person to process. I concentrate on Alice, the PER life, and can feel myself kind of oozing into it, it's hard to explain, but I can sense it, tingling, throughout my body.

Could we have sex? Or will it be like at the end of our marriage, that is, will I hump away and think I'm doing a good job but look down and see no expression at all? Embarrassing to be thinking this but it's been so long. And what if she got pregnant? Would it be a real baby or an image of a baby? Ghost baby, dream baby. A half-reality fantasy infant unable to live in its structure. I need to relax. But I'd be lying if I said I didn't want to try and see what would happen. I need to sleep. Alice isn't on the concrete steps anymore. Could a PER baby breastfeed?

Alice never wanted to have a baby, but I think in those early years she considered it. I wanted to but became scared. Another fault in my generation. Having babies isn't hopeful anymore. It's too much time away from thinking about ourselves, a life we can't imagine in our present. Our parent's generation loved to make a fetus. They couldn't get enough of the blue cigars and pink balloons, the details we now love to criticize.

"Want to go to Target?"

We're on the couch sitting side-by-side with our feet up on the glass coffee table eating tofu and broccoli. The TV is off, which is odd to look at when it's just a dark square. The one front window that can open is open, and I keep hoping to hear Elderly and his bag of cans, but there's only traffic and the deaf person singing again.

"Not really," she says looking into her bowl. "Why, you need something?"

"Maybe a bathing suit for the Fourth," I say into my plate, knowing this isn't something I would ever say or want. "I thought we could go to Lake George for the fireworks," I continue, scheming. "Or we'll be stuck here, watching the plaza fireworks."

"Eh," she says. "You had fun last year?"

"In A-ville?"

"No," says Alice, annoyed. "Lake George."

"Did you?"

Every summer we drove fifty miles north to Lake George. Early in our marriage the vacation was fun because everything around us – American flags flown off the back of a Harley, the DILLIGAF store, beach fireworks at 2 am – didn't phase us. We stayed in a smelly motel with concrete beds and stayed up late on the patio with everyone else drunk, mostly the shirtless of New Jersey who every year took over the town and by holiday's end crashed their SUV's into parked SUV's. Even though our intimacy was fizzling we attempted to do things married couples were supposed to do.

But if this Alice is referring to the last year we went to Lake George it means we're on the cusp of our marriage ending, when everything – arriving too early to check-in, agreeing on a restaurant, the DILLIGAF store, the flags, the midnight fireworks after getting into separate beds at 10 pm – was an argument. This isn't unusual in a marriage. Just the natural progression when the force field has been whittled away.

Before the accident my parents stopped vacationing because the trips were a closing vice of stress. Married for thirty eight years, and each year their fighting increased over wrong turns, nose-whistle breathing, too much silence, hogging the bathroom or going to the bathroom "too many times," what spot on the beach, where to eat, who should go shopping, what to eat, what to do, when to sleep, an endless and awful list. One time Dad had to turn left into this seafood restaurant but the oncoming traffic was bumper-to-bumper. He was patient. Not thirty seconds later and Mom said she would have driven up the road, turned around, and gone through the side entrance. It's what he *should* have done. I felt sorry for him in the ticking of the directional signal. At my young age, it was horrifying that a man who paid the bills, fixed everything in the house, always drove, was a cop who upheld laws, could be so powerless. He still tried to turn but no one would let him in. Mom said to just go home.

Their generation is a different one than ours, where sticking it out, staying together in gloom's grin was important. Alice said she wouldn't be like them, life is too short to suffer with another. But I would have stayed. Suffering alone is just a different color.

"Last year?" I ask coyly.

"Fucking awful," says Alice, and I stop eating. "Remember the guy who crashed his SUV into a parked car and drove away? That other guy tried standing in the middle of the street to stop him and got hit? He like, spun around?"

"I remember," I say. "The people in the room next to us played Kid Rock. All night."

"Oh shit," she says surprised in a high-pitched voice and turns sideways, her bowl now on the couch. "I forgot about them. The wife kept saying, "Shut up, Michael" to the husband on the beach every time he talked."

"And he kept doing that creepy laugh."

"Yes! He kept going *heh heh heh*," she hisses, raising her shoulders, imitating the Beavis laugh, "every time he was told to shut up. He couldn't say a sentence without being told to shut up."

"That was their entire relationship," I say satisfied with the insight.

"Shut up, Michael," scolds Alice.

I eat a fork-full and with my mouth full ask if we fought.

She holds up one finger to indicate she's also chewing. "I mean, we agreed to never go back."

Scientists recently discovered concentric circles of two-inch tall sand mountains on the ocean floor. Each mountain had a seashell. No one could figure out how they were made or who made them, but the scientists assumed it was hoax, similar to those farmers in Nebraska with their crop circles.

The scientists said the sand was crafted in a mechanical way, like a machine or hands from a diver. They did this big investigation with hidden cameras lowered from boats and a night vision camera caught the artist – a male pufferfish, three inches long, who spent twelve hours fanning the sand into the hill pattern circles, topping them with seashells like jewelry or icing. When the female approved they made babies in the clearing just before the tide washed them and the structure away.

So before bed I run a bath for Alice with surrounding candles. Maybe I won't lose her, just feels like it, if this really is final year Alice. I'll talk to Dorian tomorrow. If my gate continues in a way where time doesn't move forward concerning Alice then maybe I can preserve this life. The thought of another fallout destroys me. Into the bath I throw a chalky soap-ball costing nine dollars and it foams and bubbles, turning the water flamingo-pink. On my way out of the bathroom I turn the lights off because that's what you do in a scene like this. I've seen it before in a movie.

Sometimes I'll struggle to remember the date of the accident, but once a month I'll think about this Richard Gere movie where he walks in on his wife, Diane Lane, in the bath. Gere stands at the open bathroom door holding two glasses of wine in one hand and says, "Room for two?" Whoever wrote that line should be shot. The scene has tension because she's been cheating on him, that very afternoon, with her book-collector boyfriend who drew a heart near her vagina which she can't scrub off quickly enough as Gere approaches with the wine. You think there's going to be a colossal argument. But because Richard Gere is romantic, and he's Richard Gere, he dims the lights, which makes Diane Lane smile because now he won't be able to see the heart drawing.

"What…is this," says Alice. "It's like a spa, but in a Motel 6."

"I was trying to be romantic."

"That's the problem," she says, squirting a line of aqua-hued toothpaste onto her toothbrush. "You're *trying* to be romantic. You have to *just be* romantic."

"Right."

"There's a difference," she mumbles while brushing. "Pretty big difference."

I blurt out that I love her.

"Did something change?" She spits into the sink with force and with the way the sink is shaped some of the water hits me. "I love you too," she says smiling, but looking concerned.

I don't care what people say, when you hear "I love you" it's pure power. Years before I met Alice I worked three months at Home Depot and every contractor-husband told me to never get married. But then there was this one guy in carpenter jeans splattered in paint who said, "I bet every one of these guys complains about being married." I nodded because he had been reading my mind. He said marriage was the best thing to ever happen to him, best thing for men in general, the wives are the ones who suffer.

I get undressed and take the flamingo-pink bath alone.

My phone is ringing from a private number. Some people don't like answering these calls, but I do. Those who work telemarketing jobs have hearts too. It's a difficult job because when one person hangs up on you the auto-dialer just goes to the next number, so you never get a break. I know this because when the State needs volunteers during election season they ask my office and we're pressured to say yes.

Most of the requests never made sense. They would have us drive three hours to L-ville and have no work for us to actually do. The paid volunteers were already there finishing up. Or we'd spend five hours driving the horrendous flat route to B-ville to make phone calls in a campaign office more dorm room than professional political operation. When Steve said we could have made the same phone calls back in A-ville, he was given more phone calls to make. The campaign managers worked around the clock and during election week wore diapers.

In the beginning I always said yes. I volunteered hours of my life to politicians I never met. Once, a guy on the phone who I was inviting to a spaghetti dinner at a firehouse told me to, "Fuck the little face." He had a thick accent, and the insult didn't make sense exactly, but it was effective. Another person said to volunteer for something that mattered. That one really stuck because on the next call I had tears in my eyes.

I went door-to-door asking strangers to vote for so-and-so. Houses you don't live in always feel like they are pushing you away, but most of the time people weren't home. Entire neighborhoods of empty houses, people out working just so they can afford their home. Sometimes I would look through the narrow glass next to the doors and see a family eating dinner. One time a guy answered the door with a lizard clinging to his sweater and didn't speak. Even as I did my little speech and asked questions he was silent.

This call is from Jim, who says he's married to Rebecca, they live near the mall and have four children, all girls. A personal touch is vital. During my volunteer days you had to use your first name, never a full. Be casual. Be relatable. The most common question was why the Governor was driving around in a Corvette when the State was $64 billion in debt. A pretty good question. Our instructions were to say the Governor's personal expenses are his finances, not connected to State finances, and to add how classic cars were essential to American culture. This was printed on little scraps of paper, but I never read from it. I just said the guy liked shiny cars.

"That's nice," I say to Jim, getting comfortable on the couch, head on pillow, legs stretched out. When Alice comes into the room making a "Who is it?" face I shrug. She walks into the bedroom and closes the door.

"Rebecca," says Jim, "sometimes gets carried away like all hell." I play along. "I know what you mean, Jim."

He's all nerves, whispering. I get the feeling he works in a huge office, surrounded by others in identical cubicles.

Now it sounds like he's walking, maybe moving through the office to a conference room, like I did when I'd call Alice from work and talk for hours.

"Are you married?" he continues on script.

"Yes," I say. "Happily married."

"So you know what I mean." He pauses. "I guess I don't know how to say this, I'm sorry," he says, so quietly, it's eerie.

I sit up. Alice is still in the bedroom with the door closed. "Wait, what's this for again?"

The phone is put down, maybe rubbing against a moving leg, before he says, "I found an old flyer about your dog."

Since Alice appeared I haven't thought much about Rudy. Another effect of PER, mentioned during the training, is erased sections of your reality. What the film can't cover can be taken-away to make room for the gate. So no matter how hard I think about Rudy running at the park, he's pixelated and chopped into floating pieces.

But PER can't erase past feelings. My heart speeds up as I bring Rudy into cloudy focus over the baseball field while talking on the phone to a stranger named Jim. Rudy's transparent tongue, seeping with blood, hangs over my face.

"Listen," says Jim. "I can't talk really because she's in the kitchen, she never lets me be by myself, but she's the one who broke your car window. She's nuts like that, all hell. Like, I'm hiding in the garage right now, that's how bad my life is and, for the record, she had no idea your dog was sick. By the time she got him to the vet it was too late. I told her not to bring that damn dog in here. God, I'm sorry but –"

I ask how he found the flyer.

"I work at Rapp Road landfill. One was stuck to the door of the mall bin. Rebecca never said a thing. Why do I stay with her? Anyways, I felt like you should know. She's coming for me."

I ask where Rudy is buried.

"The vet on Pickett Ave," whispers Jim. "They cremate them too."

They're mopping the floors and the lights have been dimmed, but I'm knocking on the door anyways. The assistant from before is spraying a bottle of poison-yellow liquid onto a steel cage on the counter. With a white rag he cleans the metal bars and they shine. For a place so full of death it sure cleans up at night. I knock on the glass in annoying taps. The assistant puts down his spray bottle and walks to the door shaking his head.

"No more appointments," he says through an opening in the door. "Call in the morning."

"It's Rudy," I say, like in the past week he hasn't seen a thousand animals. "The dog," I add, for clarification.

"I'm sorry," says the assistant, putting one hand back on the lock. "We open tomorrow at seven."

If you would have told me, when I was eighteen years old, I'd be nearly forty-years-old living with a fantasy wife and knocking on a vet's door, in the dark, about a dead dog, I wouldn't have believed you. I wouldn't have believed you if you told me I'd live my life working an office job, dreaming of retirement. But life doesn't care if you work hard or live morally or have dreams. Life does whatever it wants to you.

Mom said she never trusted a person over the age of forty because they had experienced too much nonsense. When I told her I couldn't trust what she just said given her age, she locked herself in her bedroom for the rest of the day with her animals and blared Guns N' Roses. That about explains Mom before the accident. How Dad was able to deal with her I couldn't understand until I realized she was the way she was because she had to deal with Dad. It was the nonsense and absurdity of him, of being together, those summer vacations, his detachment from others including her, filling her up, shutting her down, for good.

"The dog with the bleeding tongue," I say desperately. "Someone brought him here. An angry woman, named Rebecca."

The assistant opens the door a few more inches, takes his hand off the lock, and sticks his head into the opening. "The dog who smelled like trash?"

"Yeah. Can I have his ashes?"

I follow the assistant to a back office with mahogany framed degrees from three different community colleges and a 1996 Chicago Bulls poster, the one with Michael Jordan hugging the trophy and crying. It smells like wet fur in here. The desk has loose stacks of papers, a miniature fan, and a Dennis Rodman figurine with green hair. On the floor next to a garbage can is a stuffed dog in a red sweater with white stitching on the back: PAXSON. The floor gleams like a hospital. I think that's the point – for people to arrive with their animals and feel like their pets are on the same level as a human being. As the assistant rummages through the papers the more it smells like weed.

"My boss's office," he says, moving around the desk and flipping up the papers. He reads from a sheet before reaching for the next. Behind the walls many dogs are barking. A plastic ball with a bell inside rolls past the door and a cat follows. "Hey, Rudy's here," the assistant says, excitedly. "I mean, not *here*, but here."

He flops down in a black leather chair on wheels and rolls himself to the side of the desk, legs spread wide, and pulls out a drawer from a filing cabinet helping support the desk. The drawer itself is the entire filing cabinet, endlessly deep, and inside are rows of mini Ziploc bags, each one with black Sharpie marker indicating a date, each one with animal ashes resembling pencil shavings.

Walking his fingers up the rainbow edges of the bags the assistant makes kissing noises. His eyes widen as his face scans back-and-forth. I want to vomit. I should have stayed home with Alice who, being here now, doesn't feel real. But it did happen, I know she is there. I am both in my gate and my reality and it's blissful and awful. Is this how Aidan and Lucy felt? The assistant raises a bag to the ceiling light and says, "Here we go."

I carefully pinch the bag at the rainbow edge and thank him. The bag can't weigh more than a few ounces. Rudy as a palm full of black dust and pulverized bones.

The assistant leans back and throws an orange Nerf ball at the ceiling. "Thirty dollars," he says catching the ball before throwing it again. "And you have to sign forms, like a bunch. Sheryl doesn't really need to, but she tracks *everything*. Or you could give me forty, and no forms?"

I text Alice: "Still out be home soon."

She doesn't respond.

I have exactly two twenties in my wallet.

◎

I'm driving at night with dog ashes on the dashboard. I'll either bury him at the playground or the woods behind my parent's old house. I can't keep dog ashes lying around my apartment. I don't believe in burial for myself, but doing it for Rudy is important because no one did a thing for him when he was alive. So many animals are buried in those woods behind my parent's place, and I don't want to imagine what kind of legal action I'd face if I'm found burying him at a playground. Old house it is. When I turn the wheel, I do so slowly, watching the ashes, easing on the breaks.

I pull into the neighborhood of big homes with lighted drive-ways that no one can afford, but it's fun to pretend. In America no one real sees your debt so you can be whoever you want. What's that quote... "We are what we pretend to be, we just better be careful what we pretend." Marcel Duchamp? Lights for your driveway staying lit as you dream. I pass two men in reflective vests walking four dogs. Ah, yes, the suburbs.

I'd be lying if I said being here doesn't remind me of the accident. It comes flooding back in bloody colors. If I can speak openly about the podium incident, then I can speak openly about it. I drive pass two more people walking dogs, their flashlights crisscrossing higher-up on the pavement, floating briefly over my windshield.

For months after it happened I would become either angry or depressed if anyone asked me about it. But if no one asked me about it for a stretch of time I would randomly start talking about it. It was an accident. Unusual because a drunk driver turned onto an off ramp, going in the wrong direction, and struck the only car exiting. All that glass. It was every news story because the drunk driver was an ex-Leader with a great smile, much beloved and ninety years old. He had a drinking problem no one talked about because he was charitable. My parents were occasionally mentioned as the people in the other car, but they were just an oddity, a pairing, "at the wrong place at the wrong time." I became so used to telling the story it's like how people discuss the weather. Why do some people say, when the weather is nice, "I'll take it?"

Where they were hit is an off ramp in downtown A-ville where on the fractured wall of a parking garage someone painted two gigantic bluebirds. Fractured because the spaces between the floors created massive rectangular openings in the bird's bodies. I could have painted those birds. Not really. I like to think whoever did that painting did so in memory of my parents even though I know that's not true.

The woods are accessible from a back road. Walking in with Rudy in my pocket, the light in my old childhood bedroom designed with *Family Guy* memorabilia is on. A woman with perfect posture is sitting at a computer, probably watching *Family Guy*.

I step through the woods, lots of stars in the sky above and insects moving below. Trees between houses feel out of place. Should be the other way around. I'm about a hundred feet from the house, but who knows exactly, all I know is that if I can see a woman in that room, she can see me in the woods ready to bury some dog ashes.

I forgot to bring a shovel, but I don't have to dig deep. How is the earth deep enough to bury everything once living? The sky is better off if heaven doesn't exist.

And it's not that I don't have to dig too deep, it's that I don't want to dig too deep. This area is a hidden graveyard of dead pets, and the thought of unearthing Lizzy or Bibb or Foxy or Helio, a decayed half-paw or tennis ball sized skull is unsettling.

Using my hand in a little clearing of dirt, I scrape enough surface away to sprinkle the ashes in, swirl it around beneath the brightest star in the sky. I do an okay job but not great. In the distance, a leaf blower. People who own homes think those living in cities are fucked-up, but the suburbs is a different angle of weird. I don't want to live like them, but I would if it was with Alice. The woman in the *Family Guy* room closes the blinds. I should say a prayer, but I just nod at the dirt and give my silence.

I speed walk to my car, stepping over branches and through ivy and weeds, and into the dim glow of the suburban lights. These houses make everything around them darker. Someone walking their dog is standing across the street, watching me come out of the woods, their flashlight a tiny sun held to the pavement.

"Where the hell were you?"

"I went out," I say nonchalantly. "You know, for a drive. I texted you."

"No you didn't."

Alice is brushing her teeth again, which means she either ate something after I left or something is off in the gate. Alice repeating as Alice. Everything is identical to before when she was brushing her teeth before. Not déjà vu, but a feeling more accurate. A feeling that this is, without a doubt, the same experience. The tub contains the flamingo-pink water and the candles are lit again. I act like everything is normal when Alice repeats behind my back, "It's like a spa, but in a Motel 6." She says this while I'm looking in the bathroom mirror, washing my hands in the sink, and what I notice, what it looks like, is that her lips don't move.

"But where did you actually drive to?" she asks. "You didn't do or get anything?"

Early in relationships these types of questions are never asked, but later, one person always asks them. This is final year Alice for sure. I look her up-and-down for some physical inconsistency, a glitch in the gate, something, off.

"Just drove around," I shrug, "to clear my head."

"In a circle?"

"Yeah," I say spinning in place. "In a circle!"

Alice is asleep next to me in bed. Time is passing and there is nothing I can do about it. I want to stop my life and be in the black hole with Alice. I don't want to enter the void alone, but there isn't any other way, we're all leaving at split intervals. Do people who buy lots of things think they can take that stuff with them? In some countries when you reach a certain age you give everything away. Death cleaning. At the end, it's just you, naked, waiting in an empty room.

I count to twenty and life moves forward. Alice is here. Alice is here, Alice is here, Alice is here, Alice is here, Alice is here. The air from the open window turns cold. Alice is here, Alice is here, Alice is here, Alice is here. She rolls onto me and rubs her face into my neck. I can't move, because Alice is here, her legs moving apart and to the sides of my hips.

Her hair sweeps my face as she moves her lips to the other side of my neck and it's pure skin-on-skin sensation, thrown forward into the darkness with my hands holding her ribs. However impossible, make this last forever, because I don't care how smart anyone is, all secrets, the world, are with Alice. I pull her into me by her shoulders, kiss her forehead, and it's everything.

She's trying to tell me something. I can't understand what she's saying. She speaks in a low grovel and it sounds like *Dooooorrrrr* or just *Oooorrrrr*, but what it really sounds like as she sits back, eyes closed, skin coated with sweat as the wind consumes the room: *Doooooooriiiiiiaaaaannnnnnn.*

# JUNE 27

My office building is all water. It shimmers like an ocean. Ascends with each cloud dolloped into the sky. I ride the elevator in a single whoosh.

The office floor is a desert road bordered with burning cactus and cubicles. Dorian stands on a Xerox, holding a firehose, extinguishing the flames. My coworkers aren't here, just me walking, sand-waves blowing over my feet and under their cubicle walls. Strips of clothing cling to my skin in the dream, and it ends with me in the Zone, only my head and computer visible in the surrounding wreaths of smoke and blue static dots.

I walk in on Alice making soup in the kitchen. Steam billowing up from a metal pot. She says it's for a refugee potluck lunch at RISSE, but it's not soup season. I'll pretty much eat any type of soup if it's hot enough. Let's face it, most soup is just hot salt anyway, and as long as it's hot, you'll eat it. Listen to me. Ridiculous. Happy with Alice this morning moving around the apartment tracing crescent moons on my face, kissing my shoulder, saying deep shit about immigration, telling me, "Have a good day." Who cares what Alice this is or how long she will last or what she was saying last night.

Bell's white Dodge Charger is parked up the street. The driver's side window is down with his forearm resting on the frame. Cops can have tattoos now. They like to wear short sleeves to show them off. But Bell is clean-cut as they come, he's just an egoist who likes to admire his veins in the sun. Closer, I watch his beady eyes in the rearview mirror.

"Vincent," he says, twisting himself from the car, standing then walking to where I'm about to pass on the sidewalk. "Anything?"

"No," I say, still walking. "Nothing to report officer."

"Call me if you hear anything," he says forcibly.

"Sure," I say, more to the air in front of me than to Bell. Something creepy about him I can't describe. I bet he's hairless. Dark stories in that head of his. Weird stuff he's into late at night.

"Good boy!" he shouts as I create distance between us.

At a green light, a woman in her car is clutching the steering wheel while two shirtless men clean her windshield with newspapers. I didn't notice it at first but the woman is sobbing, her chest against the horn. The men climb onto the hood and start humping and moaning and mock-licking the glass as she shakes her head. Bell's white Dodge Charger zooms up with the lights on.

Settled in the Zone, I complete three hours of data entry while my coworkers debate if Muslims should be executed. I don't know where Sarah is. She has an instinctive knack for knowing when these conversations take place and leaves to move her car or walk around the plaza or sit in the cafeteria. On her computer this morning she was staring at a full-sized add with yellow text: 99 CENTS OFF. When I asked her if everything was okay, she just nodded and mumbled, "99 cents off."

Since Alice came back, I haven't paid attention to the looting and violence, the increased fires set to convenience stores, mosques, anything appearing ethnic. The men cleaning that woman's car looked Muslim, but who cares, there are a thousand other things to worry about. I'm listening to my coworkers because I can't lock in. The general consensus is that every Muslim could be sent home today, and when I say from my cubicle that their home is where they escaped from, Steve exclaims, "Not my problem." He adds that he believes in solitary confinement, and Michelle contributes, "Do the crime, pay the time."

I don't say anything more, numbers crowding my screen, gold watch blinking. They all agree that Sarah is an exception. In my silence they hatch an idea that one commercial flight or even a very large boat could "fit them all." Emily attempts to start a new conversation by confessing she hates everything pumpkin. But seconds later they're deciding where Muslims should live.

I'm having a problem blocking them out. I'm having a problem locking into the Zone and not speaking a word.

"Alice is back," I say in my professional voice, walking into the center of the room, plucking blue M&M's from the snack table.

"The band?" asks Emily.

"My ex-wife."

On Steve's computer – a man with a purple hockey jersey pulled over his head absorbing a flurry of uppercuts.

"We've decided to get back together," I add.

"Whoa," says Steve clicking on another video, this one a zoomed-in slow motion shot of a fist landing squarely into a face, the nose puddling into itself.

"Good for you," announces Sarah walking into the room.

Telling them about Alice is the only way to change the subject, and I'm sick because it doesn't feel real, or because I have to keep eating M&M's if I want to keep talking like this.

"Well, would you look at that," says Emily from her cubicle.

Emily just a voice expecting a response without looking at a set of eyes. Emily, who loves purple and tall horses. Emily, who is marrying Otto on a day in Vermont that will be absolutely freezing because they booked the ceremony for early October which everyone thinks is autumnal but it never is, it is too late, come on Emily. Come the fuck on. Emily, who anticipates Friday and tells you about it. Emily, who sits a foot from her monitor telling us that Sears is closing two hundred stores, can you believe it.

I say hello to Francesca who after the cupcake incident and pizza party disaster wants nothing to do with me. I am dead to her. She disrespects you by avoiding eye contact and answering everything with a curt single word. But earlier this morning I decided to buy into the coffee club, even brought some into the office. I smile, holding two Folgers Dark Roast containers like weights above my shoulders. According to the labels, I've paid twelve dollars for four hundred and eighty four cups of coffee.

"Welcome to the club," says Francesca, sitting down at her desk.

She looks at the monitor over her glasses, types a little. She's wearing a red blouse with a dark stain, square shaped, between her breasts. I pour myself coffee.

"Little stain," I say, brushing my own shirt.

"Where?"

"The center section," I say, pointing at her chest. "Water, maybe."

She looks down and then slowly raises her head, pursing her lips. "It's the design of the shirt," she says, typing again, faster and louder this time. "It's Liz Claiborne."

"I'm sorry," I say.

I need some answers about my reality so I decide to take the elevator to floor twenty.

On the way, the elevator stops on floor sixteen. A square shaped woman in a leopard print blouse walks on. She doesn't notice me, so when I move past her to get off on floor twenty she screams.

## PER / SUITE 2037 / BLOOD

Using the phone outside the locked door, I tell Fang Lu I'm here to talk to Dorian and he hangs up. The feeling I have is that I did something wrong. I call again, letting it ring and ring before the State operator picks up, who I hang up on.

I call again. This time, as the phone rings, Fang Lu is coming toward the door in a speed walk, appearing more nervous than I am. It looks like he has a phone in each pocket, or maybe just weird muscular thighs. How does anyone have enough time to lift weights? He apologies. They are extremely busy.

"Is Dorian around?"

"No. What's up?"

"I have a question about my gate."

Behind him, Billy Krol is sitting in his cubicle on a modern leather chair, cardboard boxes scattered around him, most turned on their sides and empty. The office has never looked complete. Billy Krol swivels back-and-forth in his chair, one hand resting on the keyboard as he stares at the monitor. Some ceiling lights have recently burned out, allowing narrow cones of darkness to appear on the carpet. I'm surprised Fang Lu doesn't let me in, he just stands with the door open behind his back.

"He'll be back tomorrow, but keep going with everything you're doing," he says. "Your work output is high and happiness levels are solid."

"I am," I say, grinning.

"Then why are you here? Didn't you watch the video?"

His tone is condescending, and I'm not sure if it's because he doesn't want to be bothered, they really are that busy, or he just wants me to leave because something greater is wrong.

"I wanted to know how real this is," I say in a half professional voice. "I know she's not the actual Alice, but it feels like it, and I just wanted to talk about it some more, like, how long will it last? It can't last forever. When is he back?"

Fang Lu exhales in one long breath, and it makes me slightly relaxed as well, like two people making each other yawn. I get the feeling this is a move he does often, he knows what he's doing. He closes his eyes, does a few more long breaths, and says with no sense of irony that he's centering himself.

"If you're happy, why does it matter?" he says, exasperated.

"But for how long?"

Billy Krol is listening now, turned in his chair and facing the door with his khaki legs spread wide.

"As long as PER is functioning in the office, then, it's up to you to continue with the repetition schedule and mindset. We don't do follow-up screenings because they're intrusive. Data entry and screens will never change. After we leave, a maintenance plan will become available."

I don't know what to think. It's not hot in here, but I'm sweating.

Billy Krol shouts, "It's all good!"

"But the testimonials, like, what are they doing now? You don't care if they're still inside their gate?" I ask, stammering.

Fang Lu does his breathing exercises again. I'm breathing with him. On the last set he says "Flower" before the inhale and after the exhale "Fire." Then he opens his eyes and rolls his shoulders back. "Our goal is to open the gate, increase productivity, make the client happy, that's it. Then to the next city, the next town, the next group of workers. No negative feedback has ever been gathered so you don't have anything to worry about."

"I'm just worried it won't be –"

"I'll tune up your watch," interrupts Fang Lu. He opens the door behind him a little more, gesturing with his hand to come in.

Dorian's door is closed so it's just me, Fang Lu, and Billy Krol beneath the artificial lights in the center cubicles with too much empty office space surrounding us. On his laptop, Billy Krol shows me my work output during the fifteen day training and it's unbelievable. A chart shows how my efficiency compares to other workers (one is Steve, as the poorest example) who weren't suitable for PER. There's a drop-off since the opening of my gate on June 23, but not much. I'm a productive worker saving the taxpayers money while living a cheerful life.

Fang Lu plugs in my watch to his laptop and shows me more charts with increased serotonin levels as thin blue lines rising and a long string of light-gray numbers associated with chemical compounds I've never heard of. The waterfall logo turns off and on in the bottom right corner. They both agree by way of non-stop head nodding and tech-speak that the program is functioning normally. Alice as Alice is strong and vibrant.

It's hard to argue with numbers and charts if you don't know anything about them, so I agree. Fang Lu kindly suggests I go back to work. He begins his breathing exercises again. Billy Krol rolls his eyes.

Returning home, she's sitting on the lawn next to the concrete steps. I worked late, deep in a data entry trance for six hours hoping to strengthen her life. I need to keep the gate open for as long as possible. I can't be alone again.

Drops of rain begin to fall as I walk, and one fat drop smacks the glass face of the watch and it blinks with the waterfall logo. This is my life and I need to embrace it. Become it. I wave to Alice as I approach.

But maybe my reality is too strong. This Billy Krol thought and he made some adjustments by typing away on his laptop with a sticky cord attached to my temple, but my gut reaction is that it didn't do a thing. My gut reaction is Fang Lu and Billy Krol don't do much, if anything, this ride is all Dorian, the one who knows where the program and the ride ends.

The rain marks the sidewalk in dark oblong dots. This summer has been nothing but storms with inter-exchanging pockets of humidity and cold breezes. Can't complain, I'll take it. The evening sun cuts across Alice. It brightens her head and shadows her body.

"I'm home," I say, running up the hill. "I'm here," I say, groveling at her feet, slipping on the grass.

I put my arm around her and she leans away.

"Easy," she says.

"It's sunny, but raining," I say, holding my palm out. "Weird." She tilts her head. "What?"

"Wait," I say. "What are you doing out here? How did you know I'd be home now, if I worked late?"

"I'm not allowed to sit outside?"

"But why are you out here?"

She shakes a little. It is kind of cold outside, a sharp change in temperature between heat and storm, but not really. She doesn't say anything else and neither do I. The atmosphere doesn't feel so electric anymore. I can't feel the rain.

"I'm here," Alice whispers. "And I love you."

New clouds are covering the present clouds. I look forward at the rain but now I can't see anything. Another déjà vu moment. We're at the castle, on the beach where the lake is, and it's either the memory of actual Alice or the recent trip with PER Alice, I can't tell, but my head is facing the sand and she's kissing the back of my head with her lips pressed into my hair. "I'm here." "Where are you?" "All this is fakery." "Please stay." "I can't do this anymore." Everything flips. My head hits the grass. The world goes dark.

I'm inside my apartment, looking down at Alice in the bathtub with her clothes on and legs hugged to her chest. The window is open and rain is splattering the tiles. I ask if she'd like to get out, extending my hand, and she says there's room for two so I step in fully clothed and we hold each other in the water.

"Is everything okay?" I ask.

She answers, "Of course, why wouldn't it be?"

I'm making grilled cheese sandwiches as it continues to rain. I don't say a word about what just happened. Everything feels good in the present, and I don't want to knock the gate off-kilter with words. And I like the windows open during a storm. Let the sky to spray the floors.

In the apartment I lived in before this one with Alice, the landlord deducted two hundred dollars from my deposit for water damage. He sent the reduced security deposit with a bill highlighting *Windows left open during numerous rain showers, troubling.* I wasn't surprised because he was paranoid and materialistic. He wore his car keys around his neck on thick twine. When he unloaded bags of fertilizer from the trunk of his car one summer he locked his car, only ten feet away, each time after he placed a bag on his shoulder. But I don't think he was that strange. Everyone knows that landlords are the devil's semen.

"I'm starving," says Alice.

As she makes tea next to the stove I flip her sandwich. It sizzles when some cheese drips onto the pan. With the spatula I wrist-flick the cheese out and into the garbage. I have moves when it comes to pan frying. I don't use a spatula to turn over the sandwiches, I use the fucking plate.

"Nice," compliments Alice.

"Thanks."

As the cheese melts, the rain stops. What just happened between being outside with Alice and the bathtub with Alice? Maybe another glitch in my gate. Don't question it, just be happy with your happiness. Just move forward. But I keep looking at her expecting some problem, like her arms twitching into static as she pours tea. In some way, everything is normal. I shake the pan a little.

"Almost ready," I say.

"About time."

My phone lights up where the sun doesn't touch the counter and it's Alice calling. I stare. Alice is calling and Alice is next to me. I turn and smile and then go back to my phone, which like always is on silent.

"Who's that," Alice asks, and I don't know why I say it, but I say it, I say, "Alice."

"Very funny," says Alice.

The screen rings bright 518-944-4139 with Alice in New York, a picture taken shortly after we got married. We were up early and walking the city when everyone else was asleep. She's standing against the closed rolling metal doors to a bodega storefront, a painted mural on it with a baby tugging on a river in a jungle.

162

I took about a hundred pictures until Alice said, walking to me every few shots to check my work, it was the right one. I haven't seen this picture since the divorce, the paperwork question, but here it is. Mercifully, it stops. Then she calls again and the picture comes back brighter than ever.

"Can we eat?" asks Alice standing over Alice calling. "I'm so hungry I could eat a baby."

"What?"

"What? I'm hungry."

"You said a baby."

"Yeah," she shrugs. "I thought, what would be the absolute hungriest a person could get."

"It's ready," I manage to say.

"A horse isn't hungry. Now a baby, that's hungry. Could you imagine?"

She takes a cup from the cabinet above the counter where my phone is still illuminated with her name, number, and picture, but doesn't notice it, just takes the cup and fills it with water and goes out to the living room and clicks on the TV, which sounds like more news, another fire, more destruction, residents are leaving, too much sadness for one person to absorb.

Finally, the call goes to missed and I delete it. I have no idea why Alice would be calling me because she doesn't need anything from me. It must have been a mistake, but twice, two mistake calls seems impossible. Maybe another glitch between PER and my reality, the film momentarily blown back by my memories of Alice.

From the living room: "Someone vandalized The Falafel House."

"What's that?"

"The Falafel house!"

I'm a total mess. My ideal life is complicated.

◎

She knows I'm hiding something so we get into an argument. Another downfall in our marriage was that I kept secrets. I never told her about Sarah. I never told her about napping in my car during my lunch breaks. I had days at work where I didn't do any work, but if Alice asked me to take out the garbage or wash the dishes after work I said I was too tired from work. I never told her about masturbating in socks.

"Is something going on?"

"Nothing," I say, "just tired."

I remember once at the A-ville museum we were looking at World War I posters. They had this exhibit for one week only, and those who were bored or liked war went to admire the intricate line-drawings. One poster was about female spies and the headline read: "Silence Is Safety." A snake-shaped woman in a trench coat blew cigarette smoke into the words. Alice pointed and turned to me and said, "That's you."

"Because you're tired?" Alice pries. "Or because you want to avoid me? I think you want to avoid me. You shut down when you have to talk about anything real."

I'm not thinking clearly so I say, "None of this is real."

During arguments I like to stare at the floor. I sit on the edge of the bed waiting for Alice to respond and concentrate on a line, a thin trench dug into the hardwood when I attempted to move the dresser by myself. At work, Courtney told me when her boyfriend dumped her for a cashier at Target she rearranged her apartment as drastically as possible, as a way to erase Chad. She suggested I do the same. It wasn't a bad idea. But I only managed moving the dresser which created this dig in the wood.

Alice is gone.

◎

"Hello?"

There's this sound, a thumping against wood, in the apartment with me. Maybe it's Alice leaving because of what I said. The gate slamming shut. It doesn't make sense, I feel like I'm re-creating scenes from a movie I've seen years ago, but I sweep my arm under the bed and I search the closet, pushing my hanging shirts against the wall. I peek out the bedroom window and across the strip of grass dividing the houses. One of my neighbor's shirtless kids is at his window pointing a gun at me. I look toward the backyard but I don't see Alice.

I enter the hallway and call her name.

In the nine o'clock hour the apartment is dark and dreary after another storm, but there's still light left in the sky, a last line of day clinging to the underside of clouds. The thumping gets louder. It accelerates as I walk into the kitchen.

There's one weak light on above the stove, it's part of the ventilation system, and Alice is sitting on the counter next to it, banging the back of her head against the cabinet.

"Don't do that," I plead.

"Then tell me what you're hiding."

"I'm not hiding anything," I say. "Everything is fine."

She hits her head faster and harder. It's so dark in the kitchen, even with that weak little light on. There's a terrifying tempo to the way she's striking her head on the cabinet and it's painful to watch.

"Come on," I offer, reaching out to grab her, but I don't actually move forward. I have good intentions, just no good action. Add it to my list of holes in my bag. I thought I was doing better. "Alice, please."

"What's going on?" she says. "What's happening with me?"

This time I do move forward. Breathing heavily, she rests her hands on her knees. I take another step forward. She places her chin on her chest and in a spring-loaded movement her head shoots backward, cracking the cabinet's center and breaking it from the hinges.

She doesn't stop. Her rhythm is pure violence as she continues, faster, harder, her facial expression tranquil as her hair moves around her shoulders, faster, harder, the storm breeze coming in as she destroys everything behind her, the cabinet's contents tipping out like an earthquake or wraith-like reckoning sweeping the air. Eyes open, fixated on me, she has no reaction with each hit, cups rattling off the shelves and cracking on the counter. I lunge forward and grab her by the shoulders and she convulses backward, her mouth expanding with poison-yellow froth.

Her skull bounces off the counter's edge as she slips toward the floor, as I fail to hold her.

"To the living room, anywhere, let's go, you're real, okay?"

Onto the floor calling me a liar, saying she deserves better, head crashing into anything that will break with her force. She dents a floor tile and blood splatters outward like a firework. Calling me a loser. Someone with only a past. Telling me to leave her. Telling me to divorce her.

*Do not control the gate.*

I pin her to the floor.

*Let the gate guide you.*

Her head rests to the side as if falling asleep.

*Do not confront the gate about its plausibility.*

I don't want this anymore.

*Do not attempt to escape the gate.*

But I have nowhere else to go.

*Do not question humans inside the gate.*

But I have no one else to concentrate on.

◉

I run and grab a towel from the bathroom. Back in the kitchen, she isn't here. Where she sat on the counter it looks like a grenade went off. The splintered cabinet door is on the floor leaning against the stove and most of the cups and dishes are broken or badly chipped. Smeared blood leads from the shelves, to the counter, and down and across the floor.

I search the apartment.

A buzzing sound is coming from the bedroom.

The gate opening back up, the gate shifting, the gate so imperfect.

I walk into the bedroom.

Alice is asleep in bed with no sheets. She's curled up in a fetal position and shaking. Quietly, I walk over and inspect her head and find not one cut. I run to the kitchen again and everything is fixed and in perfect place like nothing happened.

*Documenting the gate by video or photo is prohibited.*

Fuck the gate.

# JUNE 28

Bell is calling while I'm at the grocery store buying prepackaged spaghetti and meatballs for Francesca. I figure it's a way to apologize for everything I've done or not done in the office lately. This morning I left Alice sleeping in bed, still not one cut or sign of what happened last night. I'm not sure how many hours she should sleep, but she needs the rest, the recharge.

I haven't called Alice back. At first I had no desire to do so, but now I'm thinking about it. Last night was a nightmare. Alice is not sustainable. But maybe? No, I don't think so. I'm happy in my life now. Maybe the gate will correct itself. It's still early. But I need the real. No. I'm happy in my life now. Yes. I'm happy in my life now. I'm happy in my life now. Things are just a little... fucked up. Things are just a little... hole-heavy.

"St. Peters," states Bell. It sounds like he's driving with the windows down. I bet he's in short sleeves again. Running red lights because he has sirens. You would think with everything happening in A-ville he would have more crucial things to do, but I'm not surprised, I once saw a cop riding a bike down a hill past a burning bodega.

I turn around an endcap with 2 for $4 bags of Doritos. An employee is stuffing the shelves with unbelievable speed, slicing boxes open with a box cutter, throwing the bags onto the shelves slightly faster than the people pulling them off. It's a great deal. But what the employee is doing alone is amazing in its proficiency. He's a machine, it's art, but no one records him.

"Peters," repeats Bell, slightly louder, the phone cutting out. "The old man there. Spent...found at the park. He asked for you. There? *Hello?*"

"Yeah," I say, but my head is crammed with Alice, the thought of her as impermanent, something withdrawing, someone I have no control over, someone or some *thing* with the option of leaving.

I get in line as Bell continues to talk, but I can't hear him with all the wind blowing into his phone. It takes a second for me to realize he's telling me where Elderly is.

The man with the blood-red suspenders, Caesar Salad, is here again, holding, what else, a Caesar salad. What you have to realize is your circle is very tight, a radius of five miles or so, and the same people are inside this radius performing the same tasks as you. In my radius is Alice, coworkers, guitar playing neighbor, pizza eating squirrel, deaf person singing, Shawl Lady, Bell, Dorian, Fang Lu, Billy Krol, Elderly, Rudy above RIP, and Caesar Salad. Who am I missing? Someone or so many? Those in my radius including myself are on repeat, and when we're gone new people will replace us, doing similar things.

During my painting "career" my favorite film was *The Exterminating Angel* because one scene is dinner guests entering a castle twice. You think it's a mistake, a glitch in the film, but it's just the guests re-entering their reality again. This is what life feels like to me, hoping to crack through and into something else, another chance, another dimension, but you're just doing the same moves.

"Thank you," I say to Bell.

"For?"

"Telling me where he is."

"Not much of a favor," says Bell, and the sirens come on, which means either an emergency or he wants to zoom through a stop sign.

I decide to do something strictly against the guidelines, that is, call in sick to work and go to the hospital. I lock in on Elderly. I shake everything else from my head.

My routine will be compromised. I won't complete the suggested daily data entry, my face into a computer so important in the maintenance, the headset, the water, the watch flashing with light and logo, but I need to see Elderly because it feels like one of those defining moments, and if I don't show up I won't be able to live with myself. My imagination of what could have happened to him will only be worse. Besides, I can get back on track with PER, Dorian isn't even around. Also, the Alice problems are glaring, and if the real Alice is trying to reach me maybe full reality is possible again.

I leave the line at the grocery store, place the prepackaged spaghetti and meatballs into where the rotisserie chickens stay warm, and the guy stocking the Doritos gives me a big thumbs-up.

I walk across the street to the bus stop. I wait in the summer-heat under a metal awning in front of a smashed CVS sign. Taking the bus is faster than walking to my car, I think, or just running. It's so hot outside it hurts. The bus is approaching in the near distance, sagging to the sidewalk with each stop. Quickly, I email Francesca while standing inside someone's vape cloud.

A shower curtain is pulled across and around where the bus driver sits. Light-blue with slits of white rain, the curtain is hung above with plastic laundry clips and twisted metal wires in a half circle.

On the floor, big army boots and a ring of garbage. I pay my fare and find a seat.

I love public transportation, but can't remember the last time I rode the bus. Like a library, it should be free. Another one of Elderly's ideas, so good. Taking the bus feels right to go and see him. He'll appreciate it when I tell him.

A huge man wearing a suit with the dress shirt cuffs covering his hands sits in a wheelchair behind the driver, the wheels locked by tiny chains to the floor. The man takes up so much space it's hard not to stare. He appears naturally a part of the wheelchair. His face is perfectly shaven and shellacked in sweat, tortoiseshell glasses resting low on his nose, mouth parted in a stunned expression. I'm sitting slightly behind him, but on the opposite side, facing him.

"The Body," says the person next to me. She leans over when she speaks, and means to whisper, but she doesn't, she's loud.

"Hey, I know you," I say, unable to believe how truly small my radius is. Out the window the sky darkens to a violent purple. The first raindrops smear across the glass.

"I'm going to talk," she says rolling her shoulders back, "but don't you dare say you know me."

"We work in the same building. We ride the elevator together."

"I've ridden this line every day for three weeks and The Body is always on it," she continues, adjusting her shawl. Her green flats are dirty now. On her lap is an open purse showing three prescription vials. "I'll tell you one thing, if I was in as bad a shape as him, I wouldn't go to work. But I guess it's inspiring? I've taken hundreds of elevators. Big deal."

"Who are you?"

She shrugs. "Wait a second," she says, now excited, "he's going to do it."

I shift over, but the seats are designed to cradle an ass like mine, so there's only so far I can move, I'm kind of stuck in the mold.

"Wait for it."

If you don't have earphones or a book to read on the bus you look like a fucking creep in these sideways facing seats. You have to stare out the window or pick at the skin around your thumbs or read old texts on your phone. How do you get a job as a bus designer? With Shawl Lady, I look out the window, but we're really looking at The Body, waiting for something, whatever she means, to happen.

"I know," she continues, "you don't believe me that he's going to do it. But just a few more minutes and he'll do it. I'd bet you a hundred dollars if I had it."

I look out the window.

His spine becomes rigid like he's being electrocuted, head wrenched left, toes diving into the floor. One thick neck vein pulsates as he tries to control his body, the instrument of his torture. Whatever he does it doesn't work, the wheelchair bounces like we're racing over potholes, chains rattle, and something inside him squeals.

The driver says, "You got this, Earl."

Shawl Lady's elbow nudges my ribs. "Told you he was going to do it."

"Remember what we talked about yesterday," says the driver. "That this too shall pass."

I hate life.

I love life.

I just want Alice back.

The rain comes hard, and The Body stops, his head hung, he appears to be sleeping, his muscles zapped of energy, the cuffs of his shirt touching the floor.

"Works for the State," says Shawl Lady. "Never misses a day."

"Pretty depressing."

"No," she says pressing her purse into her chest. "He's completely out of his mind. He's both on the ride and off the ride. Oh, you didn't hear that from me. Sitting at a computer all day doesn't necessarily feel like it? Not too shabby. Here's my stop. And listen, you're little secret is safe with me. I'm not telling him because I'm rooting for you guys." She stands by gripping the metal pole, pulling herself to her feet in a smooth motion. "Also, you didn't speak with me today, yes?"

The bus travels across town, away from downtown fires and through the suburbs where the streets are named after renaissance painters. On one side of the hospital, the police training academy, and on the other side, a law school with a bad reputation. Each brick building has sprawling front lawns fenced-in by black iron gates. The sun illuminates everything into the unreal, which, given my life, feels right.

Everyone – the sick, the visiting the sick, nurses and janitors, an entire community – exits the bus at the hospital. I rarely watch the Leaders when they're on State TV, but one time I remember a Leader's mouth saying there were two types of people: those who are sick and those who will be sick. They wanted to pass legislation making it illegal to have six hospital beds in a room designed to hold only two, but didn't have the votes.

I'm riding the elevator with four men in lab coats holding trays of blood. One is a surgeon, and wears one of those thin caps shoestring-tied in the back, but this one isn't hospital-green, it's the colors of the flag. I step off on floor ten and start looking at the room numbers, searching for 1008.

The hospital – the lighting, nurses station, the cream colored walls and flower paintings – is identical to an office, if you swapped out the beds for cubicles, made slight adjustments to the layout. But it has the same feel. I hate this realization, and being here reminds me of Mom and Dad. I didn't need to visit them, that's true. I didn't need to see Dad connected to that red machine pumping air into his lungs. I didn't need to see Mom attached to a wall of wires.

Elderly is sleeping under fuzzy blue sheets. They've cut his hair and shaved off his beard, a few red nicks from the razor on his jawline. His hospital gown is tied neatly around his neck and there's yellow lotion on his skin, little dunes of it under his eyes. He looks waxed. If it wasn't for the hospital setting you could dress him in a suit and give him an office job. I imagine, when he arrived, someone said to clean him up, look at this bum, or maybe a new hospital program to have the sick look their best possible and this is the result, which isn't Elderly, but someone else. I feel sick. On his wrist a purple bracelet says FALL RISK and a yellow one DO NOT RESUSITATE. Under the sheets, one ratty blue arm sticking above and against its head, is his stuffed animal named Millionaire. Standing over Elderly, I carefully pull Millionaire up so their heads are touching as they sleep. I'm still capable of sentimental things.

I plop down in a leather chair. I should call Alice. I work myself up into a phony confidence I once channeled during conference calls. What is Alice doing right now? Does she even exist when I'm not there? Maybe she only appears when I open the front door. Maybe my body near her is the trigger to her appearance.

On television is an ad for a salad spinner. Then a local news story with a masked protestor throwing a garbage bin through a Bank of America window. Everyone thinks in twenty years we'll be living in a dystopia, all storefronts blasted out, banker's heads on spikes, but in twenty years I just think that no one will care. The protesters will give up when they learn how powerful and indifferent the State is. Good people become corrupt with titles. I'm being negative again, but I've seen cruel things done by friendly politicians. So much wasted money, and they love to breed.

I'm not calling any Alice.

The nurse sneezes as she slips the needle in. After she leaves with the vials of blood, Elderly opens his eyes. He leans forward and looks toward the door. "She gone? I like to pretend I'm asleep when they do it."

"E," I say, and put my hand on his leg.

He leans back. "You know what I could really go for?"

"What?"

"Big burrito."

In a hospital you order breakfast by pushing numbers on a phone. As he pokes each number with a way too long press, he says he had a heart attack in connection with poor blood circulation. "Well," he says, casually, "Omar thinks my feet are kaput. I don't know what they're going to do about them, but they seem fine to me, they still work like feet, just don't look like feet."

Sitting up, tugging the blankets at his thighs, his bandaged feet are stump shaped, and it's enough for me to understand I have no power, nothing I have or could say will help this situation, could have helped Mom or Dad, I was just there, like I'm just here.

When I was a kid you had to put your time in during family events even if you didn't want to be there. Birthday parties lasted eight hours. A hospital visit was a day trip. It was more about obligation than love. I don't know which one I'm acting on now. I don't know when, in my existence, I've known why I'm doing what I'm doing. Some people can run off a list of personality traits describing themselves, and at a young age know what they want to do for a career. They know what they want in a house and car. I've never known. Once on a home show I heard a guy tell a real estate agent, "If it's not Craftsman style you can forget about it."

"I was running in the park," continues Elderly.

"From?"

"What do you mean *from*?"

"For exercise? Someone was chasing you? Was it someone from PER?"

He folds his hands on his chest. "The body is a temple, V," he says condescendingly, "and you have to condition it."

"Just thought –"

"I have a gym membership."

"You do?"

"I don't."

A fat calico cat slinks past the room. Elderly says it's Graves. That if she naps in your bed after midnight you don't wake up in the morning. She comes in to either comfort you as you ascend to heaven, or take your soul to hell, according to Elderly.

I could believe him. Everything makes sense if you let it. Someone once looked at the stars and saw an eagle, twin boys, a crab, a woman falling.

"A cop told me you own four houses," I say hesitantly, "and that you're married."

Clean shaven, his hair styled like a little boys school picture, he doesn't look anything like Elderly. "If you don't have someone to love houses are traps," he says.

"But you are married?"

"Martha drives a Lexus," says Elderly. "A Lexus SUV."

"Is she here?"

"Fuck, I'm tired. What is this junk?" He yanks weakly on a tube inserted into his forearm. Around the needle a piece of clear tape unsticks. "What's going to happen to me? Never mind, don't tell me."

"I could ask. Want me to ask?"

"No, it's better not knowing. If you see them tell them I don't want to know."

He doses off again, his mouth open and drooling.

I leave the room. Graves is walking the perimeter of the hall so I follow. In one room the lights are off and tied to an empty bed is a silver helium balloon with the number 95. Graves walks in, leaps onto the bed, and curls herself into a comfortable ball on the pillow. I keep walking. In another room I see a child in a reclining chair holding a Dinosaur coloring book. But most of the rooms are empty, beds curtained off, a biohazard bin in a corner, beeping machines, a crucifix cross on each wall. Even with the curtains open the rooms feel cold and terrifying.

At the nurses station I ask to speak with the doctor treating Elderly. All the nurses chew gum and have ponytails and tired eyes brightened with make-up. If I had a daughter I would tell her: You will meet very few people in this world who love what they're doing. So the trick is to be one of the few that has something inside them that needs protecting, but don't let anyone else know it, just keep doing it, protecting it, letting it grow and giving you meaning.

A tall doctor, not too dissimilar to the veterinarian who treated Rudy comes walking down the hall, shakes my hand, and introduces himself.

"As his son," says Omar. He guides me into a lounge area, off to the side of the nurse's station, with enough space for one family.

A TV sits in the corner on a Formica table. The news is on. More protests. More buildings curtained in fire. It doesn't feel real, and I wonder if it's PER, the fantasy covering what I'm experiencing and not working the way it should be. My reality could be poking holes through my film, but there's no way to know without talking to Dorian.

"No, his neighbor," I say, declining to take a seat. "He asked for me through Sergeant Bell."

"Who?"

"Sergeant Bell," I repeat. "The police."

Omar sighs and flips through a chart. "Has no family and lives in his car, hmm," he comments. "Maybe a month left, difficult to tell with circulation. Think you could convince him to live in one of the homes until hospice? His wife doesn't seem open to any possibilities." He closes the chart. Then he steps too close to me and peers into my eyes. "Sir, have you been drinking?"

"I don't drink."

"Your pupils," he says, turning his head. "Highly unusual color and dilation. Would you mind?"

"I would."

Two nurses who have been talking about skin grafts are now looking at us.

"Five minutes. Just take a seat over there and I'll check your blood pressure," he says, grabbing my wrist and guiding me toward a room.

"Please don't touch me," I say nervously. "I'm late for work and it's extremely important I get there. I need to get to work because I have work to do, at work. Don't you understand?"

I'm starting to sweat and trying to use my professional voice, but it doesn't sound like me. Inside my own mouth my words echo. "I have to do my work today," I continue. "I have to go to work because I have to, I have to do my work. I have days that add up to my retirement, and if I miss those days I won't have any retirement." Those visiting loved ones are walking from their rooms and into the hallway to watch. "It's important, you know. I have to go to work. I have to be at my computer right now. Don't you understand?"

"Of course," says Omar, releasing his grip. He does the slightest of head shakes to a security guard approaching from down the hall.

"Thank you," I say.

Omar keeps his distance following me to Elderly's room. On the way I nearly trip over Graves, I have to do an awkward legs-apart jump, and from one of the rooms, someone, only legs packed in ice visible on a bed, claps.

I walk into Elderly's room, tell him he's going to be released, and say that I've found Rudy.

"Lying is important," he says, his head compressed backward into three soft pillows. "You have to have liars to make any of this work." He waves his hand around the room to signify the "any of this" and sighs. "Thanks for the cans, V."

His food arrives via a bald man in all white hospital scrubs with an American flag pin over his heart. The tray is placed on a swivel stand then positioned over Elderly's lap. Taco salad. The bald man unfolds a napkin and begins tucking it into Elderly's collar. It seems humiliating, so I'm surprised when Elderly smiles, exposing his neck.

Elderly asks about the training, and I tell him it's Alice, all I see is Alice. I say the real Alice is trying to reach me, and I'm not sure what to do. Alice, I confess, isn't exactly Alice. I'm not directly asking Elderly for advice, but it comes across that way.

"That's funny," he snorts, and blinks slowly. "There's no way out."

"The Tehran workers," I say, placing my hands on the edge of the bed where his legs are. "Were they happy?"

"For a little while," he wheezes, "but like everything else, it wore off."

"I thought there was a connection between them and what's happening with PER."

"Why? Because you wanted it to?"

"I just thought."

"V, I don't feel so hot. V, I know where all this is going. My age, where I am, I know."

With a napkin I wipe his chin that is covered in salsa and lettuce strands. He seems to have no feeling in his face. I tip the plastic cup of water at his lips. I adjust his pillows and the angle of the mechanical bed and I sit and put my time in.

I adjust his blankets when he says he's cold even though it's warm in the room.

I itch his leg where he has an itch that he can't reach.

The last story he tells me is how he once saw an old friend's name in the obituary. He walked five miles in a snowstorm to the wake. When he arrived he realized it wasn't his friend, just someone with the same name.

Francesca asks why I'm here when I called out. As I pour coffee I flatly respond that my stomach is better. If you want to dominate an office power-shout, "Good morning!" when you walk in, and if you want to skip a day, say you have the shits.

Basically my email was that I needed a large amount of time to sit on the toilet. Disgusting, I know, I don't like it either, but it works because no one wants to talk about what the body is capable of. So much shitting.

"Just be sure you correct your time sheet.," says Francesca. "I heard the last one had mistakes."

"Thank you," I tell Francesca. "Thank you very much."

"No, thank you very much."

I'm in the Zone, head woozy with the day. I texted Alice I need to work late again. Settling into six hours of data entry will strengthen the support beams of my gate. What's unusual is that she doesn't respond. People looking at their phones look depressed and I'm sure I'm no exception waiting for her response, especially sitting in a cubicle. The little gray cloud with the flashing three dots appears, which means she's alive and typing.

I texted the wrong Alice. It's an easy mistake, given PER Alice was never saved in my phone, only the previous texts that I deleted. The real Alice answers with a long stream of question marks and, "Just wanted to say I'm coming to A-ville. Why won't you answer?"

On more than one occasion I've fantasized about throwing my phone from an office window and here's another.

My first reaction is to text back, "Wrong Alice." My second reaction is what if they met, PER Alice reaching out to touch Alice. I stare at the picture of her in New York in front of the bodega mural. I slip my phone in my pocket, decide to go to floor twenty and get Dorian's opinion. Maybe this has happened before. Once again, I run away from the real.

Dorian has his feet up on his desk with a picture of Ronald Reagan on his thighs. A salad more bleu cheese than greens wilts in a plastic container next to his laptop, a screensaver of a fighter-jet ascending with silver and gold exhaust. The carpet is filthy with lunch crumbs and coffee stains, and the windows, which I thought were locked on every floor, are wedged open with tiny wooden blocks, a warm breeze blowing through and flicking the corners of papers. He doesn't say to sit, but I sit in the same spot as before, during the interview.

"The best social program is a job," mumbles Dorian with his thumb on Reagan's hair. "As a person with a job, do you believe that?"

I don't want to answer because I want to ask about Alice. "I don't know, but my gate –"

"Right," he interrupts. "Everyone who participates wants *things*. Why are you so different?"

"I'm not sure," I shrug.

"Well, you're not the first. We had a woman before who saw birds. I'm serious. Her entire house just covered, inside-and-out with birds, even splashing around in her sink." Dorian smiles sadly. "Tremendous worker though. But it's okay for you to continue. I don't see any real serious problem. That's why you're here?"

"There's something else."

"I have to tell you something. We don't plan on staying much longer. We've been *very* successful. The best social program is a job. Be honest. Do you believe that?"

"I don't understand," I say. "It's over?"

He says they've hit their quota for participants, the office is full (I didn't see a soul on the entire floor), not much for them to do now but sit and monitor. He shrugs in a manner to convey boredom. He has the drained expression of someone who has achieved something, relished it, and is now waiting for what's next. C-ville is their next stop which he doesn't seem to care for. He says Fang Lu and Billy Krol have already begun the screenings. He says pizza in C-ville is lasagna, but I don't laugh or try to correct him.

Each time I try and speak he interrupts me.

"Pizza," he repeats, "like lasagna."

He's in a good mood looking out the window while discussing his marital problems. But when I finally cut him off to tell him about the real Alice contacting me, there's genuine concern. His expression, along with his head, snaps back-to-center, facing me.

"Wait," he says. "*What?*"

"The actual Alice," I repeat. "The real one."

"Here? Now?"

"Maybe not *right* now."

"Are you seeing her? Are you planning to?"

"I'm not sure. Can I?"

"Why didn't you mention this before?"

"Because of the rules. I didn't want to mess up my gate."

I mention the phone call. How Alice must have seen the incoming call, she was standing over it in the kitchen and I said it was Alice calling. I tell him how I texted the wrong Alice. How I broke one of the rules and she tried to destroy herself in the kitchen. I describe the glitches.

He looks a little sick, physically shocked by what I'm saying, but he's interested, transfixed on everything I'm confessing, wanting more, questioning why none of this was caught by Fang Lu or Billy Krol or Kate Helms, a name I don't recognize and then realize, my heart racing, could be Shawl Lady.

He wants to know why wasn't any of this brought to his attention earlier, but too late for that, too late to worry, now he wants to know everything about Alice.

If I updated my bag of holes list it would look like:

183

- Alice
- Alice
- Alice
- Alice
- Alice
- Alice
- Alice
- Alice
- Alice
- Alice
- Alice
- Alice
- Alice

"The wobbling of the gate," Dorian says sorrowfully.

I try and smile but just exhale nervous air. "Sounds bad."

"I'm thinking," he mumbles. "My guess is you'll have to choose, but hold on a second." He opens a drawer.

I do my nervous cough. "Choose?"

"Decide which one you want. Together they could have consequences. Glitches we can fix, it's still early, but this, hold on a sec… honestly…I'm not sure what…" He's shuffling through papers on his desk now. "But I can't see, I can't see a positive outcome. Could lose both in the overlap. Wait here."

Dorian returns holding a white binder with the waterfall logo on the cover. Inside is the article I found on the internet, and what appears to be other papers he has written. As he flips through, the articles separated by some sort of color coded tab organization, there's the anime sumo wrestler Crying Sub-God with the white tear. "Hey," I say, reaching over and pointing on the paper and stopping him. "I've seen that."

He puts a finger on the sumo wrestler. "This guy?"

I tell him I received an email with the same picture after our first meeting.

"Oh, that's nothing. Krol sends it on day one of training," he says, and continues to flip through the pages while settling into his chair. "To see if you'll click on it. Participants who watch porn never access their gate."

At the end of the binder there's an article that freezes Dorian. I look away, pretending to think about something else, suddenly feeling awkward. It's odd to look out the door and see nothing but vacant office space, cubicle walls with no person inhabiting them. Either Fang Lu or Billy Krol had hung a Fourth of July banner. It's still push-pinned, one corner only on the far wall, but now drooping into the water fountain.

Dorian puts his feet back on the desk and places the binder on his lap, not to relax, but to shield the text from me, I think. He hums and touches his lips as one eyebrow rises.

"Absolutely," he says, tossing the binder back onto the desk, "too risky for both realms."

"Both realms?"

"That's right."

"What am I supposed to do?"

I think about Alice at home, how she's Alice at the end of the marriage, where the tension was so great that every sentence had the weight of a weapon. If Alice at the castle was the peak there's only a decline coming. The glitches I could have lived with.

"I think the situation," he says, now leaning forward, the storm clouds dimming the room, "is new and fascinating territory, but my concern is Alice viewing the real Alice while inside your gate, what her reaction would be in such a situation. And just the mental strain it would put on you, depending on the reaction, I mean, it's already affecting you." He smiles, proudly. "If Alice is shown herself…The interweaving of film and reality is where the wobbling of the gate, your entire atmosphere…Never had this come up before." With both hands he smooths his hair backward. "My recommendation is to collapse the gate before it's too much for anyone involved. Especially yourself."

"Okay, sure, I'll do anything."

"It's such an interesting case."

"Lucky me."

"Like something sent from outer space."

I sign a release form with the PER logo watermarked in the center. He reaches below and to the far right side of his desk and opens the same drawer and out comes the white box again. I can't imagine wearing a second gold watch, what would that look like, but I go along with it. With my arm extended across the desk he uses a twisted paperclip device with little teeth to unlock the watch from my skin. There's a burning sensation so I turn my palm up and see a dot of raised blood on my wrist. Dorian hands me a cotton ball and clear tape. If I was drugged then it all makes sense. I have a sudden flood of anxiety because I don't want to lose any version of Alice, I want all Alice. Another wave of anxiety. It's already too much for me to handle.

"It was a drug?" I ask, blotting the blood.

"Not entirely. Technology and nature combinations have yet to be sufficiently explored, but we rely on what we know to get you into the gate. Are you familiar with visual completion theory? It was mentioned in the packet. That helps as well, once the desire is located, then the repetition training is what really activates it all," he says, handing me another roll of clear tape because I can't get this one to work.

The sky is dark and dreary, and I cover my small wound. If stars had eyes what would lightning look like to them? In the distance, three columns of black smoke. Did we set a record for thunderstorms yet? I want more records in my life. Fires are being extinguished by the rain and I'm going to lose Alice again.

"A-ville," says Dorian, relaxed now and nodding at the window, "I've never seen such a place."

"It will be fine," I mutter, thinking about Alice. I've been saying *It will be fine* my entire life and it has gotten me nowhere.

"The collapse shouldn't be more than a few days," he says. "Because your training was so successful, shutting it down should be easy."

I ask how he can be so calm now. He says there's no other choice. He's looking at the Ronald Reagan picture again. "We've had to collapse one or two gates before, clients who just couldn't handle what they saw, like the bird lady. It became overwhelming. Birds stuffed in the plumbing. Birds in the water heater. Birds flattened under the mattress. Birds chewed-up in the garbage disposal. Who could live with all those birds? Plus, she couldn't concentrate on her work, a major deficiency that you didn't experience in the slightest." He sounds like a cop, a politician, a lawyer, a Leader, no emotion, no compassion whatsoever.

"But this is a person," I say.

He hands me a printed out PowerPoint slide with an lime-green background and white text illustrating how the gate will end.

The subtraction of the watch, the pills, the repetition work, all the methods, are important, but you also have to break the rules many times over for the gate to properly close. A side list is precautions to take, how to react properly to the vanishing film, which in my case is Alice leaving me again, Alice as a soon-to-be memory, soon-to-be fading into the first.

"I think we're all set," he says.

"Did I do a good job?" I ask, surprising myself at the question. It just forces its way out of me, the child-to-parent feeling of being in the presence of Dorian Blood, who seems surprised by the question as well, his face kind of scrunches up as he sits back. One time Dad said I could ask him any question in the world, I was seven maybe, so I asked what a blow-job was. I thought Dad was going to fly backwards through the walls of our house when he heard that question and I think Dorian might too. More lightning outside and more columns of smoke and fires smoldering throughout A-ville, making it anew.

"You did," he answers.


I settle into the Zone and don't do a thing because I'm not sent any work. The PER System with the waterfall logo is no longer accessible. So I reactivate Facebook, and like a hummingbird jump from site-to-site. It's so easy. I become distracted by people who don't care about me. It's enjoyable.

I need to concentrate on the real Alice. What would her ideal gate be? A $20 minimum wage, universal healthcare, a four-day workweek, no prisons, high-end grocery stores built in the poorest of neighborhoods. An ideal gate that doesn't involve herself. Is peace an option, even in fantasy, if you live here? I'm being negative again. But the thickness and strength of such a film seems impossible.


My work day is a typical work day before PER, before the podium incident. Steve, from his cubicle and directed at no one in particular says he dislikes walnuts. Yes! Michelle slurs – sounds like she drank during lunch – that you either have a country or you don't. Zing! Emily is into the Muslim ban, and how really it wouldn't cost much to charter a thousand flights to send "all of them" back home. Ba-boom! I lower my head until my forehead is resting on the edge of my desk. There's a lot of crumbs on the floor, and what appears to be a half slice of pizza. I guess ants can't make it up this far, but one time we had a pigeon stuck in the wall and listened to it for weeks. Every morning Steve would slam his fist against the wall to see if it would chirp or be silent. They cheered when it went silent.

The tape comes off my wrist, and soon after the cotton ball falls, my wrist drips blood.

I wake up to Michelle saying, "At the funeral, she laid down in the casket to take a selfie." In the reflection of my monitor I'm a self-portrait disappearing.

I'm in the bathroom and my phone is ringing from the living room. I took a shower because I walked home in the rain and my hair smelled liked smoke, according to Alice, who didn't move from the couch when I came in. I rub a glob of clear-green lotion into my palms and cover my face. All things considered, I don't look so bad.

On my walk home I considered the following: if Alice is divorcer Alice, and if PER can't handle a person as the focal point of an ideal gate, and the real Alice is coming back for whatever reason, then what choice do I have? I don't need to preserve my gate, I need to preserve my future. I need to move toward my retirement while working on my reality: the real Alice.

"What's that?" I yell from the bathroom.

Alice is talking to someone in the living room. Maybe my eyes do look odd, Omar was right, a washed-out brown, the shape too is a bit squashed or, just, off. On the fogged glass I write GATE then smear it with my fingers. Alice shouts my name, and when I don't respond immediately she shouts it again.

I walk out, rubbing lotion onto my arms, trying to act as normal as possible, and she's in the middle of the living room holding my phone out to me. I haven't decided when to begin dismantling the gate. She looks so real. She looks so alive.

"It's Alice," says Alice.

A tidal wave of anxiety washes over me. PER Alice can communicate with the real Alice.

"Hey you, it's Alice," repeats Alice.

"What?"

"Your wife," she says, tapping the phone against my hand. "You haven't been returning her calls?"

"I don't know what any of this is," I say, taking the phone like I don't really want it. "Must be a wrong number," I say glancing at the screen (it's really Alice) "or a crank call, or, I don't know. I've been getting a lot of telemarketers lately. Have you been getting a lot of telemarketers lately?"

"Stop being weird," says Alice, "and talk to Alice."

"I'm not being weird."

"Then talk to Alice," replies Alice.

I turn my back and whisper hello into the phone while walking toward the kitchen.

"Vincent," says Alice, "why won't you talk to me?"

One thought I had is that Alice previously called because one of her parents had died. Maybe she didn't have anyone to talk to who had experienced losing a parent. When we were married, her mother had a dozen ailments and continued to live through the diagnosis. They could have ganged up. But this isn't true. Alice is involved in the rebranding effort at RISSE around the corner and wants to get coffee. She wants me again. Saturday morning. She ignores the fact that herself answered the phone. Hiding in the bedroom, I say that sounds great, coffee, sure, I like coffee, great, perfect. She says, "I'm looking forward to it."

"That was Alice," I tell Alice walking into the living room. She's on the couch, eating gummy worms. My first attempt at dismantling the gate feels wrong. "I'm going to see her again."

She shrugs. "So?"

"I'm meeting Alice."

"You already said that you fucking idiot."

"You're not Alice," I tell Alice.

She gets up and walks toward the bathroom and her movements are lethargic. For a second, her left leg looks like a star-filled sky, and the skin on the back of her neck is a flaky moon-gray. I sit on the edge of the couch thinking this is it, the end, the collapse.

I run through the six rules in my head while itching my wrist.

Water is running in the bathroom and it runs for a long time, too long for her to still be washing her hands or her face or brushing her teeth. Outside, the sun is below the clouds now so it can do whatever it wants, but it's raining in the light. Everything I see in my life is unbelievable. Maybe Alice is gone. But she comes out with a towel pressed to her damp face, and into the living room, smiling like Alice, and it's impossible to believe she isn't real and will ever leave.

# JUNE 29

An electrician on a red ladder is installing ceiling lights in the breakroom. His steel workbox, open on a tray on wheels next to him, has a piece of cardboard taped to it with the following written in black Sharpie: ITEMS GAINED BY WICKEDNESS DO NOT PROFIT.

These new lights are a brutal level of fluorescent, I squint walking through the breakroom. How bright is a star close-up? A black hole actually contains color. When she leaves, will Alice experience pain? I don't want to think about it but I am. Am I doing the right thing? Is there such a thing?

At the water cooler is a little girl in a baseball uniform – sky blue shirt and white pants and yellow baseball cap with ponytail pulled through – most likely the daughter of an employee in another office. I've never seen her before. Maybe Steve has a daughter he never mentioned before, which would be a very Steve thing to do.

"Big game?" I ask.

"I'm the catcher. What do you do?"

"I'm an office worker working toward retirement."

"What else?"

Water is leaking from the blue jug and onto the floor. Standing in a clear puddle, the little girl stares at me. I really don't have an answer. The janitor with the YEARS OF ABUSE shirt comes lumbering around the corner and throws down a Slippery When Wet floor sign.

"I just work an office job," I say and flutter my fingers on an imaginary keyboard.

"I'm waiting for my Mom."

"And what's your Mom's name?"

"Mom."

"No, what does her Daddy call her."

"Sarah."

I'm walking from the bathroom and Sarah is coming out of the women's bathroom at the opposite end of the hall. I had no idea she had a kid. In an office where everyone talks about every intimate detail, she has said nothing about being a mother. The electrician is humming a familiar song, and the little girl is throwing a ball against the wall.

"Vincent, you okay?" Sarah asks.

"I'm fine."

She touches my stomach, palm flat, and leaves it there. "Okay?" she says, then looks embarrassed. She removes her hand. "I'm sorry, I don't know what I'm doing, I'm in such a weird mood, you know?"

I repeat, "I'm fine."

"Everyone in the office thinks you're cracking up. I don't know how to say it, but they're saying you're losing your grip."

"Oh, because I am," I try and joke.

"You could talk more. It helps to get stuff out. You don't have to be like them, you know."

I tell her all the mistakes I've made with Francesca which makes us laugh, even though I'm not sure it's funny. Even the electrician, his head disappearing inside a removed ceiling tile, laughs. This is how the world works, if you let it. When you immerse yourself in an office life you end up laughing at things that aren't funny in your life. And it's not unusual, millions do it, everyday.

"I don't know," says Sarah. "I just felt like I had to say something. You've been so quiet in your cubicle since coming back. I mean, you *were* quiet, but most of the time no one knows if you're here. You have such a great spot. Steve really wanted it. I got my kid back. After five years I have custody from…I'm just so happy."

"Mom, come on!"

"I have to go. I'm worried about you. Take care of yourself."

Sarah walks away, heading back through the breakroom.

I turn the corner, and a light tube is slipping from its sword-shaped box, raised by the electrician on the ladder. I start to lunge forward, mutter something, but I don't really try to catch it. The light shatters on the wet floor.

"Goddamn it," fumes the electrician. "Well, it's not my money."

"It is," I say, "it's taxpayer money."

"Shit on me. Hey, you have that corner cubicle, right?"

I nod.

"I fixed your light. Put in one of these new high voltage babies."

I walk back to the Zone.

"You look like Bert, from Bert and Ernie," says Alice when I walk into the apartment. It appears she hasn't moved today, the apartment surrounding her looks untouched. She's dressed in what she wore last night.

"Thank you."

"It's the shape of your head," continues Alice, who sits on the couch with her feet up on the table. The TV shows a man in a leather vest and American flag bandana with his outstretched arm aiming a gun at a crowd of forest-green ski-masks. In the background is a storefront framed in fire and people running in and out. Holding up one hand toward my jaw Alice pretends to turn my face in a deep study. "I don't know if it's because you're getting older, but your head is longer and has a pinched quality to it now."

"Like Bert's."

"Exactly," she replies satisfied.


She screams from the kitchen. Sitting on the floor with her legs crossed, head down, Alice is scratching at the floor tiles, peeling them up. I sit down next to her and ask what she's doing.

"I felt it from the beginning. The call confirmed it, but I don't care. I'm not going."

I wonder what hotel Alice is staying at. She could be at RISSE right now. The real Alice could go for a walk and Alice, looking out my apartment windows, could see herself. She could walk down the steps wanting to meet herself.

It's excruciating, but touching Alice I tell Alice she can't stay.

"I said I don't care," she repeats, this time with more force, glaring.

I break another rule. I agree with her, tell her yes, you aren't real. Her skin dims. Her hair flickers white, three night stars suspended in the mess. Everything is fine. I take a deep breath and she slides across the floor like it's suddenly been turned vertical. I flip onto my stomach and reach, but she's dragged into the ether edges of my collapsing gate.

I scramble on all fours and dive at her outstretched fingers.

I slap my hands along where the wall meets the floor.

Losing any version of Alice again is too much. I run through the apartment calling her name, wishing her back.


The bed covers rise with the mold of two bodies embracing. Limbs are writhing, arms and legs entangled inside. I'm seeing things, this is part of the collapse. But we're in there, I know it, those are our bodies moving under those sheets, Alice and I, forever. Before we were married, Alice and I never talked about the future. Before we were married, I woke up holding Alice. Stepping forward, I pull the covers off, but there's only the beige-bare mattress, a cloud of hot air.

I cover the apartment three times, everything to the sides blurring and shaking, and I know I should be excited Alice is leaving when Alice is back, but I'm a mess.

Outside, I do two laps around the house in my bare feet, quickly becoming wet from the grass. My landlord, standing in the corner of the backyard, waves hello. The neighbor's guitar playing is improving. A few backyards over kids on a trampoline are screaming over the low fences.

I walk into the apartment and Alice is sitting on the couch with her feet up on the table. She says, "You look like Bert, from Bert and Ernie."

# JUNE 30

Michelle said on her last summer vacation it was so hot she couldn't visit the donkey sanctuary. I check my retirement fund. I should start smoking for the breaks. I should drive to work and move my car every two hours. I should come back from lunch completely wasted and pass out in the stall.

My boss is snoring in his office, a digital Las Vegas slot machine spinning on his computer, McDonald's bags everywhere, box fan buzzing on the floor.

"A sanctuary? For donkeys?"

"They love 'em."

My boss wakes a little after two, and because he's so bored he has us draw straws to see which one of us has to stay, everyone else can leave early. It's the hottest day of the year and the Leader's staff are working from home. The Dome offices don't have air conditioning and let's be honest, there's really no work to do.

"What does a donkey even do?"

"What do you mean *what does a donkey do?*"

There's a real *Hunger Games* vibe to everyone standing in a circle in the office. Before it even starts Sarah says she will just stay, the game doesn't need to be played, but my boss says it's not an option as he walks to us holding the straws and in his other hand orange scissors. Sarah has been redecorating her cubicle with pictures of her daughter. Donkeys had a purpose, like a hundred years ago, but now they just give rides at birthday parties.

We pull straws and Sarah loses.

◉

One way to leave work is through the underground plaza, no windows, connecting the Dome to more office buildings and Mosby Avenue, which runs parallel to my normal route. On occasion, I do this when I'm tired of walking home in the same direction. Today I'm just scared. It feels like Alice will never leave. It feels like I'm doing something wrong.

The underground plaza is empty and the only light is coming from the tiny windows on the third floor terrace. It's a massive marbled space with vaulted ceilings. The chandelier-like lights are kept off in the summer months, a fact routinely publicized in the Leader's mailers. I walk slowly, repeating the rules in my head, coming up with a plan to erase Alice.

Three workers are roping off the Governor's blue corvette for a display in the center of the underground plaza. Why this is so odd is that no one is around, here in A-ville, for any event. Normally everyone arrives from surrounding cities and villages during the fall and winter months. A display is usually assembled for the heavy traffic to come, not this time of year. But I guess even the Governor gets bored.

Did you know that the ex-Governor had one of the biggest art collections in the world, and when he got bored, do you know what he would do? He'd have a helicopter move his lawn sculptures to new places in his rose garden.

In the cold air, the marbled walls and limestone floor, the ceiling easily two stories high, a corvette roped off in near darkness. The workers sip Stewart's coffee and check their flip-phones. One of the workers keeps scratching his dick. What a world. A sign printed from our office illustrating the corvette's power compared to three hundred cartoon horses sits on an easel under a spotlight.

I don't know what to do about Alice. I don't know what to do about my life.

As I head home, turning right up-and-out of the plaza toward Mosby Ave, Shawl Lady sprints, then disappears around a limestone corner.

At home there's no Alice. I call her name and check all the spaces again, do the walk around the house and come back in. Nothing. Not even a hair in the sink. Gone.

# THE WEEKEND

The sky is low shelves of ultramarine blue clouds, and fluffy black clouds of mammoth explosions rise in the higher distance. The sky doesn't even know what it wants anymore. I'm walking to a café to meet Alice. Sidewalks should be different colors. Confetti could fall for no reason at all, we don't need a celebration every time, you could just put some over random doorways and make someone's day. Life could be more exciting this way. My life is thrilling on a Saturday morning.

Sitting at a side table against the windows drinking from a white cup is Alice. She sees me coming through the door and stands up. It's her. Physically, there is no difference between Alices, but the feeling I have as I get closer is way different, a great fire breathing in my head. I might have a podium incident on my hands again. My stomach is either upset or I'm hungry, I can't tell, and my legs are weak.

"This is so nice," she says giving me a hug, "it's been awhile."

I mumble, "Yeah."

"You seem tired," she says. "Go get a coffee and then we can talk."

I walk to the counter and order a black coffee with no room. It arrives from a secondary barista, a tall teenager weighing a hundred pounds who walks on the balls of his feet. Alice is here. He places the coffee with two inches of room in front of me. Alice is here. I pay two dollars and leave a dollar tip. Four women in pant suits run into the café shielding their heads because it's raining outside and the cashier says under his breath, "Get the wraps."

"So you're back," I say, sitting down. "I mean, here we are." For some reason, I extend my arms.

"Back in A-ville," she says, wobbling her head. "Who would have thought? Not me."

"Not me either."

"But here I am."

She's in front of me and we're sharing the same air. We're in a pocket in the massively ugly world and I can finally say, truthfully, that it's real. Little circles of hell are all around us, but I'm in the comforting pools between.

"So, how's life?" I ask.

At the counter the four women in pant suits really are ordering wraps, each one with bacon, each one with a slight variation from the next, olives or no onions, dressing on the side or extra dressing in the wrap, lettuce or no lettuce, and I think of Mom, maybe all moms, I don't know why, but it's upsetting. I don't think about it for long. I concentrate on Alice.

"Pretty good, compared to here," she says touching her necklace. "You?"

"The usual."

"I figured," she says. "At least you still have that job, your retirement coming. Not the worst thing in the world."

"No," I reply, "not the worst thing."

Most of the discussion centers on what's happening in A-ville, the swarms of protesters and violence. Listening to Alice talk is different than listening to Alice talk. There's a history here, a depth that has me equally excited and depressed. Layers of life are present. I want to be back inside it. We don't say a word about the divorce.

She will be in town for the next few days. A family of five from Syria are flying in tomorrow. She kind of slips in – it's jarring – that

I should invite her over for dinner on Monday. She will be working at RISSE until five so the timing is perfect. She says she misses the apartment and would like to see it again. I've never thought of Alice as sad before, but something here, her shoulders maybe, makes me think so. "Why not? I think everything is behind us now," she says, and everything feels like clouds, doors, blown to the far sides of my reality as a new tunnel appears.

"Sure," I say, making a big dumb grin, "sounds great. You're right. Why not?"

"The woman who answered the phone," says Alice, pushing her empty cup to the side of the table, "is it serious?"

"No," I say. "Just a coworker."

I order us each a second coffee. This time my coffee has more room, about half full, and the barista smiles while saying, "Have a wonderful day, sir." He can't be more than sixteen. His name badge says Mr. Dan.

I've had too much coffee, but no one takes having too much coffee seriously. Once when I was bored at work I did hours of research about caffeine consumption and found an article about eight researches who had studied the coffee bean for twenty seven years. And they didn't come to any conclusion on if coffee was good or bad for you, but two years into the study each researcher had quit drinking it.

"We're getting jacked," I tell Alice, feeling more comfortable.

"Yeah. Look at this place," she says, glancing around.

"Are you worried…with what's going on and RISSE?"

"I worry," she says. "But I have to keep going."

"That's good," I reply mindlessly.

"Yesterday I asked a Syrian girl what she wanted to be when she grew up, and instead of saying a doctor, a teacher, a scientist, an astronaut, she said she wanted to be useful."

"Wow."

"We want to do painting classes. They'd love you. You should come over. "

"I don't know."

"You don't know if you still paint?"

Boys in suits are ordering complex drinks they don't tip for.

"I don't know about coming over."

"I'd like it if you did."

"Yeah?"

"Of course."

I agree to not only dinner at my place, but to stop over at RISSE and help with the painting class. I follow this version of my life, dizzy with Alice, high on reality.

Walking home I feel lightheaded.

Back home there's still no Alice. Nothing to do with the day but think about her.

Going to bed early. Dreams or not, my life is happening.

I wake to the refrigerator door slamming shut. I figured after coming home yesterday and Alice being gone, that was the end of her, a hologram slapped away, but here she is, dressed in yellow sweatpants and a blue tank top, moving sleepily around the kitchen pouring oatmeal into a pot of boiling water on the stove. It's difficult to tell one Alice apart from the other. But one has our history inside her. One is real and always will be.

Here's a PowerPoint slide I made last night:

- Two realms
- The wobbling of the gate
- A copy viewing itself
- Choose what you can control
- Reality can be altered
- New life with Alice

Because it's Sunday we have to do something as a couple. I suggest either the mall (Alice groans) or back to the castle (she shrugs).

I need to attack the gate. It's hard knowing that the Alice before me is going to leave after thinking she was already gone. I need to be aggressive. Without the repetition schedule at work, without the gold watch, the headset, the pills, the water, everything PER, this Alice can't survive, I know, but breaking the rules again and again will truly end it, it's just, difficult.

She decides on the torture of the mall to spend our time in. The weather is too unpredictable to do anything outside, she says, which is true, according to the news A-ville has set the record for thunderstorms in an American city. And we might break the world record, become #1, which is saying something because I read an article once saying A-ville was the most average city in the country, a fact based on various companies conducting test market research here more than anywhere else. When it comes to education, financial status, intelligence, and attractiveness, we have the most average citizens. No wonder Alice left me. I was born with A-ville written all over me. In high school I graduated two hundred students out of four hundred. The coaches moved me from the athletic kids to the kids who couldn't jump, repeatedly, back-and-forth, for years. I got married, then divorced, and now she's back. Everything evens out, not too low, not too high, in A-ville, the ideal place for Dorian and PER.

*Documenting the gate by video or photo is prohibited*

We're walking through the centered skylight spaces of the mall. I drop back on the cloud-white floor tiles, holding my phone up to record a video of Alice. Beautiful in its own way to watch in reality, but when I replay the video, following her into a store selling soap, the video doesn't show Alice, only oval shaped air heat-trembling at the edges. I replay it three times, shocked each time when I'm unable to see her.

I walk into the store. A woman in a lab coat holding a steel tray of lotions, each one in a fingertip-sized cup, asks in a Scottish accent if I need help and I say no, walking the perimeter, pretending to shop for glitter-encrusted soap. I check back around the entrance, and then back inside, smiling at both the woman in the lab coat, and now, a security guard who is suddenly present.

"Got you!" shouts Alice from behind me and slaps my shoulders. The security guard rolls his eyes and turns around and makes a throat-slashing gesture to the cashier.

"Where were you?"

"Here," she laughs. "Shopping. Where were you?"

"I was right here."

Her face scrunches up. "What?"

The skylights are now filling with summer light. If you're a child, you can drive tiny tugboats around a fake lake for a dollar, and ride a red jeep that seesaws for thirty seconds, for two dollars. The kids really like the fake lake with the tugboats. The parents like it too because they move randomly even if you don't put a dollar in, so the three-year-olds can turn the shiny metal wheels for hours and it's free.

Why didn't we have kids? We talked about it early in our marriage and came to the conclusion it would change our life "too much" which, really, now that I think about it, doesn't mean anything. What's wrong with having kids to save the marriage? Sometimes I wonder what our baby would look like, what traits of mine would it have for a lifetime. I like to think she would have a great sense of humor so very little could hurt her.

*Do not control the gate*

Alice wants to get our photos done in one of those booths located randomly around the mall. Parents are pushing toddlers in carts shaped like cop cars and the retired are exercising with two-pound weights. A woman hitting a Starbucks with a straw is yelling, "Meeting at Dunkin Donuts! Meeting at Target! Meeting at Burger King! Meeting at Taco Bell!" I think I'm in love. A man in sunglasses is walking by dragging his body along the wall. He kind of slides and slips, slips and slides, repositioning himself if he slopes too low. A Best Buy supervisor is berating a worker about her shirt that she is frantically trying to tuck in. Down a grim hallway leading to the bathrooms someone is moaning. A baby is vomiting into her mother's hands. How is everyone not screaming?

Alice tries to grab my wrist to pull me into the photo booth and her hand slips through. She has no reaction, but continues into the booth where she closes the curtain. Only her sandals are visible. She's humming a familiar song, but I can't place it.

"Vincent," she says from behind the curtain.

*Do not attempt to escape the gate*

I'm walking toward the glowing letters of MACY'S and a stage with Fourth of July colors set-up for a dog fashion show. I slide my feet on the tiles and tell myself it's okay, I have to break this rule, leaving is necessary.

Inside the pet store, a crowd of dogs press their wet noses against the glass, trying to get the attention of the dogs being assembled on the stage. The show starts in an hour and people are already sitting in the front row on white plastic chairs, their hands folded on their laps.

I make a U-turn at the MACY'S entrance with a man who looks identical to me, just older and more bald. He checks his gold watch as he completes another lap of power walking.

On my way around to the other side of the mall I notice it's raining on the skylights. For a place so interested in consumption, I'm surprised they took the time for skylights. I wish the Zone had one. Elderly could use one in the hospital. Every structure should have a skylight, doesn't seem right closing off the sky. A corner cubicle with a skylight, the sun shining down on your computer. Ambulances should have skylights.

I continue walking with the old version of me swerving through the crowd far ahead. I'm heading toward the exit. Passing the lake with the tugboats, I turn to the right and I'm back at the photo booth, Alice's sandals visible below the curtain. I look around because it's impossible. I went a different way to avoid coming back to this spot. I had a plan. I can't see where we came in.

She pulls the curtain to the side and peeks her head out. "You coming in? Everyone does a *looooooovvvvveeeee* picture."

*Do not confront the gate about its plausibility*

The seat inside the photo booth barely fits our hips. Alice has selected a space cats theme for our five vertical pictures. As the screen counts down from five, I'm into the destruction. Looking at the camera fogged over with kids fingerprints I take a deep breath then tell her she isn't real.

"Ouch," mocks Alice.

On the next picture I say this life isn't possible. She pretends to be punched in the stomach and smiles. I go into extreme detail, conference call style, about how implausible and temporary the gate is. For each light-blast of the camera I attempt to close her.

"I don't know what you think you're doing," she says as we wait for the pictures to print, "but it's not working."

The printed strip falls into a plastic scoop with a clear door. She grabs it first, says they look good, then hands them to me as she walks ahead into the colors of the mall.

In each block, each photo, there's a border with cats hovering in space wearing astronaut gear, one planting the flag on the moon, and below, in the five pictures, no Alice. Sitting with my wife, I'm alone. In the first photo I have my arm propped up and around an imaginary person. In the second I'm being kissed by a black hole. The third, no one on my lap, but I'm contorted like there is. In the fourth I'm tenderly touching heads with a void. In the last photo I'm being shoved, my eyes closed as if flinching, by hands and arms not there.

*Do not question humans inside the gate*

I walk in a daze with no Alice near. I don't know if this is a good thing, Alice gone again. I've lived years of my life doing nothing but missing her. I tell myself yes, it's a good thing, you have the real Alice to concentrate on now and put your energy into. Think about the future. Think about your retirement

The sun is shining on the wet skylights and big globs of rain are streaking away. In the food court a man sitting alone lifts his face toward the light. I stumble through the tables and chairs filled with families. It smells like Chinese food, Wendy's, and plastic tables sprayed with lemon scent.

"In the war," says the man warming his face, "Sergeant Conway called sex P-Touch. You believe such a thing? We're in Paris and he's asking any set of legs *Excusez moi, fancy a game of P-Touch?* You believe such a thing? By your expression, you don't believe such a thing. Why not?"

I'm hyperventilating, wondering what's real and what isn't. How can this man be real? How can his story be true? He's off the ride, lucky, on a different plane of joy. He doesn't need reality. Maybe Dorian had something to do with what happened to Elderly, a way for me to not interact with such a person on a daily basis. I wonder. I don't know. I don't think I'll ever know.

"Oh my, oh yes," the man continues. "Conway. Tough son of a bitch. Head like a soup can. After the war drove a forklift in a carrot factory, if you can believe such a thing. I can tell from your face that you don't believe such a thing," he says, cleaning his front teeth with his finger. "A veteran in this country is no better off than a bum. One time I saw some people chanting "U-S-A!" in the unemployment line and I tell you, truest thing I've ever seen. Conway spent years begging for money and asking for P-Touch, using baby powder as deodorant, praising Jesus, oh, the things we do. You do realize there is really nothing to do?"

*Let the gate guide you*

Through the atrium style windows the clouds are bunched in slate-gray levels, but the sun still cuts through ending in a block of shadow at the food court's midway point. Near an Orange Julius in the far corner Alice appears. She's standing motionless with her arms by her sides.

Turning around, wanting to leave, those doors are the exit we came in from, I'm sure, not really, Alice walks behind a kiosk selling discounted calendars. Alice is standing in a store trying on shoes.

The gate is collapsing.

Alice is walking into a store selling candy by the pound. Alice is crouched and rummaging in her purse. Alice is powerwalking with a group of Alices. As I move toward the exit, they all disappear. On the skylights, thirty Alices on all fours wave at me before being blown back by the wind or film yanked across the roof. I'm sweating in the air conditioning of the mall. Two more versions of Alice run past me holding hands. They disintegrate into a jewelry kiosk.

"Vincent!" shouts Alice from the upstairs level.

Alice is leaning over the balcony and her hair is falling around her face. What else, what other rules should I break to close my gate before tomorrow's dinner with Alice? I've hit them all. I've tried my best to create room for the real. I'm near the exit so I could run. I couldn't hear it during the rain, there's music playing in the mall, but why?

"Wait there," she says, "I'll come down to you."

I get through one set of doors in a burst and there's the roof of my car, blinding white with beads of rain in the sunlight. Alice comes through the door to my right extending her hand to my face. "Hey. You okay?" she asks, slightly out of breath. "I said wait up."

Maybe PER Alice is messing with me, but a man is holding the second door open, not for me, but for her. "Oh, I'm good," she says, and he lets go of the door, irritated. I love my life. I hate my life. I ask if we're still on for dinner tomorrow. She says of course, why would it change. Her head tilts. She asks if I'm feeling okay, mentions my eyes, and I say yes, I'm fine, thank you, I'm fine.

At my car with my keys in my hand I look toward the mall. The only person at the entrance is a tiny man in denim with a sunken chest, bent in half, holding a metal walker.

I'm not one for dramatic emotions. My parents, when forced to hug someone after a family gathering, used only their upper bodies. Feeling like crying, I never cry. Finding out Pluto wasn't a planet was depressing. Never slam dunking a basketball, of course. A horror movie has never made me scream. When I was a kid, Dad took us camping on an island and I got lost. I thought it was the end of my life, but I didn't scream. I sat under a tree for hours until he found me. But I scream, a kind of embarrassing yelp, when I get into the car.

"Never do that again," says Alice, reaching over and starting the car.

"What's that?"

"Disappear like that." She puts the AC on just face, full blast. "What's going on with you? What's going on with us? The weekends are torture. All week I dread the coming weekend because I know you'll be there, chewing. I hate my life because you've trapped me in A-ville with your job. I could have done things. I'm smart you know. I *was* smart. Now I just stay home and feed you. I fucking can't stand it."

Her shoulder is translucent and inside is a swirling storm of stars. If I look closely enough I can point out all the constellations I know, which is every single one.

"But what about RISSE? You wanted to do that," I say as I reverse the car. A family of five in T-shirts holding Best Buy bags pass by in the rearview window.

"For a few days a week, yes, thank you for reminding me," she says, sarcastically. "Thank you for telling me to be happy. But I couldn't take the promotion because of you. I couldn't do what I wanted to do because I'm with you."

Instead of arguing, I drive. I've experienced this Alice before, and I sense this Alice ready to explode further. Everything she is telling me she has told me before. She keeps talking and it all hurts, the Alice of those closing months still alive.

Driving northbound, the highway on the southbound side is on fire in one football field length section. We drive silently under the weaving ramp system with trucks above hauling poisonous goods.

A block from home we pass a construction site with ten men in orange vests staring into a sinkhole. "It's unbelievable," she says into the window, "that everything is built by men."

# JULY 3

During a holiday, workers receive the day before off, and sometimes, the day after as well. Very typical State worker benefit. Hundreds won't work this week, and the ones that will won't have anything to do. They justify not doing anything by saying to themselves that at least they showed up. But I don't know how I could get it so wrong and actually come in without realizing, last Friday, that Monday was a vacation day. I blame the nightmare weekend. I blame my life for fucking-up my life. It's a minute past nine and I'm going home.

Before leaving, I walk around the office. For the first time ever I enter each person's cubicle without them. An office with no one inside it is so quiet. It feels impossible a human ever inhabited such a place.

On Steve's cubicle wall he's hung a small banner RESPECT THE FLAG with an army ranger on one side and a person dribbling a basketball on the other. Three empty mayonnaise jars are positioned behind his monitor. On top of the jars are Diet coke cans stabbed with pencils. I circle his mouse and the screen lights up. His desktop is a picture of him holding a shark. I push the delete button on his most recent email.

I keep going. Michelle has a job she hasn't seen. The Governor needs a banner for his corvette display. I delete that. I go through her drafts folder, so many partial emails directed at her Lexus dealership, about how much she likes driving a Lexus. When she feels the timing is right she will purchase another Lexus, just, now is not the time.

It's thrilling to alter reality so I delete more.

I stand in Sarah's cubicle and look at the pictures of her daughter covering her cubicle walls. One is them in the underground plaza, smiling next to the corvette display. She has also put up older photos of when she was a girl standing between her parents dressed in black burkas, the background all desert, a distant flag with green stars.

Emily's cubicle smells like baby wipes. Several red white and blue Yankee candles and a large container of lotion. A tray of half eaten Lindt chocolates. I find her favorite horse picture, the one called Princess, and just before I delete it, I leave it.

In my boss's office I shred the time sheets. I find papers listing gambling debts where he owes unpayable amounts of money. This office life, there's no fantasy here. I turn his computer on and delete emails, barely looking at the sender or subject line. It doesn't matter, I just want them gone.

I delete and delete and delete.

I disconnect Francesca's keyboard, which will confuse her for hours later this week.

I get carried away. I go back and delete more work files that will get everyone in trouble. Any incoming jobs vanish. If my boss has any negative reaction, or really, any reaction at all, it's when a Leader complains about a job not being fulfilled. And if the job isn't completed, and the Leader, or staff, doesn't remember the job, and the Leader doesn't complain, all the better. It's work that doesn't need to be done.

I change my mind when it comes to Francesca. I walk into her cubicle and look at her family portraits. She has framed her computer monitor with flag stickers. I find a drawer of Post-It notes, the ones she doles out by single stacks and tracks. Around her computer are endless job slips needing filing, too much work for three people, let alone one, and other papers my boss wants photocopied for no reason besides creating work for her. I find a calendar where she tallies how many pots of coffee she makes each day and how much of her salary, so minimal and insulting to begin with, she spends on coffee. Written on the back is a budget for what she pays for each person's birthday. She has scratched out Emily's surprise party and written next to it *RUINED*. On a Post-It note I write *You deserve more* and stick it dead center on her monitor.

The weekend wasn't enough time to erase Alice. I head to the elevator to go see Dorian. Give me advice on collapsing the gate, Blood, before the real Alice appears at my door.

Disconnecting from the program and breaking the rules isn't working. I could tell the real Alice to meet me somewhere else, but having her in the apartment again is crucial. It will spark what we had before, if she sees what she left behind.

Shawl Lady is in the elevator again, her chin on her chest, shawl draped over her head. What I don't do is compliment her shawl or say anything about the bus ride. Some people have experienced great traumas in life. When one of the holes in my bag was fear of driving over a hundred miles per hour, it leads to bouts of immobile road rage. A car would zoom by, cut me off, and take a sharp turn into a church. And Alice would say, "Maybe someone they know just died, ever consider that?"

So sometimes it's better not to say anything at all. Shawl Lady doesn't acknowledge me and I don't acknowledge her.

The security door at floor twenty was deactivated – no red or green light on the black pad. The main room where Fang Lu and Billy Krol worked is empty with the exception of a cubicle wall – no thicker than an inch, but six feet high, seemingly hovering in the

215

center of the room. How it's upright with no support on either side, nothing fastening it to the ground, I don't know. The slightest breeze should knock it over, and here it is, standing.

I walk a circle around it. The blue carpeting I step on has paper-clips and crumpled pieces of paper, a piss-colored power strip lays coiled up against the vents under the windows. The blinds are up, and for miles it's storm clouds swirling.

I knock on Dorian's door. He doesn't answer so I go in.

Nothing in here but a desk and balled-up Post-It notes and the box of broken glass, which has been moved from its previous spot and is now leaning against the garbage can. He probably figured the janitor would empty it over the weekend or today, but didn't consider the holiday. HQS never works the weekend before a holiday. HQS dislikes work in general. Five years ago they converted a storage facility into a self-described man cave, napping and selling weed while collecting overtime. The story was all over the news. Here's something else you need to know when it comes to the State: a part of your taxes is spent on someone else's vacation.

The box itself is about two feet long and a foot wide, more of a top to a box than an actual box, I now notice, and the glass shards are skinny triangles stacked in layers. Something is glowing at the bottom. Slowly, I pull the glass out, piece by piece, placing them on the table.

At the bottom are typed sheets, yellow and crusted in spots like liquid was poured on them. Carefully, smelling them first (no odor) I place them side-by-side on the desk.

I start reading. It doesn't quite make sense at first, but there's an order. I re-arrange the pages, leaving squares of moisture on the desk.

Holding the papers, my hands shake. It's a follow-up report on Lucy and Aidan, the participants featured in the training video.

Neither, says the report, was unable to adjust back to a normal way of life after their gates collapsed. They were, "unable to perform daily work functions" and were fired. The conclusion is that mentally they just couldn't adjust to reality after experiencing their ideal life.

Three suicide attempts in as many years listed in Lucy's report, and mental health records for Aidan, endless prescriptions from specialists who couldn't get him out of bed. No other follow-up reports are in here. Maybe the others are still in their gates.

It doesn't matter to PER, because once the gates are established, there's no money involved. A single page of expense reports is included. A-ville is the only place so dysfunctional and average to ignore the warnings. Money, when you run a program like PER, exists when you receive the initial contract from the State. What Dorian leaves in his wake, according to this report, is only temporary, completely unsustainable, lasting weeks, maybe months, then it's back to your stupid life, which you can't function in.

Unless you can transition from your ideal gate to your ideal life. Unless you can move from one Alice to another Alice.

In the elevator I hit the button for the ground floor, and when the doors close, I hit the button for floor eighteen, the Shawl Lady floor.

The doors open and I enter a bright hallway with flower paintings hung on the walls. It's an identical set-up to my floor. As I move down the hall the flower paintings become smaller, beginning with sunflowers, ending with roses.

I walk into an open room of cubicles, one at the entrance, three in the middle, one in the far back corner. A Xerox in the direct center has the cord plugged into a ceiling outlet. All the lights are off, the only light comes from the windows. The floors uncluttered.

Where I sit at in the Zone, located on my floor, someone I can't see is typing. I'm surprised no one has designed a silent keyboard. Seems obnoxious everyone has to hear your work and feel your productivity.

There are zero personal touches, the cubicles only contain a computer and chair in the relative darkness.

The Xerox clicks on, hums, and begins printing pages. The typing stops, I don't move, then the typing begins again fast and fluid. I glance at what's printing – difficult to read they are shooting out so fast and sideways – but at the top right corner on each page is my name, date of birth, and social security number.

Angling my head, viewing twenty pages or so I read a bulleted report of my weekend activities. There's my coffee with Alice on Saturday and my trip to the mall on Sunday. Details like what I ordered at the cafe, when I laughed, what I tipped, and how I acted at the mall (*talking into thin air, walked in circles, did one of those photo booth things*) when multiple versions of Alice were present are written in shorthand followed by small symbols and strange code.

A page shows the numbers 1 through 20, ascending and then descending.

A page shows how the gate will close.

Is Shawl Lady recording what I'm doing as I'm standing here right now? The typing stops. Maybe cameras are everywhere, pill boxes with a microscopic lens in every corner. But I'm not doing anything but thinking, re-reading the page showing how to kill Alice. Everything in my life is impossible. That's not unusual, everyone thinks that, and how can billions think that way and still think we're each unique?

"Hello?" says Shawl Lady. "Dorian, honey?"

I think she's going to come out of the cubicle, but instead she starts typing again. I walk out of the office so slowly and head to the elevator. I know what I have to do now. There's no door to make noise but I think about sneezing, and as I'm leaving, she's typing.

In the elevator I hit the button for the ground floor. The doors close and I'm falling. I sit on the floor and pull my thighs to my chest and shake until the doors open. Head up, I'm faced with rain.

"I don't care what happens," says Alice, standing on the coffee table. She's wearing a black robe with bees on the shoulders and sunflowers down the back, a cream colored bra, my blue mesh shorts. She kicks a ceramic mug off the table and against the wall, spraying it with coffee. The ceiling seems lower as I search for cameras. My head is spinning. Alice is still here and Alice is coming over. Turning back around, the coffee seeping down the wall is disappearing like washed-out watercolors.

I mutter, "This isn't easy for me," which doesn't mean anything, I just want to respond. This isn't about me. It's about gaining Alice while losing Alice and considering what Alice wants in life. Divorcer Alice said I viewed her not as a person, but a pliable piece in my reality, a thing to place meaning onto and it was unfair. It *was* unfair. The story's center was always my viewpoint of her with me. I'm a bag scattered with a thousand holes all labeled Alice.

"Go ahead," she taunts. "Go ahead, whatever it is you want," she continues, pacing from one end of the table to the other, which only allows two steps. "Whatever it is you want to do."

I break the six rules in thirty seconds. Speed is the requirement.

There's lightning just outside the windows as she crouches, covers her ears, and screams. Everything vibrates. Everything begins losing color.

I smash the gate again and again as she fades, torso transparent, lungs faint-blue bags heaving, hands each a night sky pressed to her dimming head of stagnant white smoke.

I stop and hope this is it, one Alice leaving and another about to arrive. A-ville leveling my life out. But she comes back in vicious vibrant color.

"Let me see her," she pleads. "I don't care. Let me see what I look like."

I start going through the rules again and her body flickers, static-like, then moon-gray, before coming back, but this time incredibly faded. At the mall she didn't look scared, but now she does.

What I'm doing isn't finalizing the collapse that should have taken place by now. I need another plan. "I'm staying until she comes through that door," warns Alice. Escaping right now is a rule I haven't concentrated on, so I run to the bedroom, grab what little paint and brushes I've kept in the closest over the years, and head to the door with Alice, half-clear, still on the couch, hoping by the time I come back this will all be over.

"Vincent?"

She's standing at the front door of RISSE. Behind her is a hallway with wood floors. A room off to the right contains a circle of children playing. To the left, an office with a man in white pants, white button down shirt and gold rings, swiveling back-and-forth in a chair, reading a magazine on his lap. As I enter, he looks up with eyes only and exhales.

"I brought my paints," I say. "You know, for the kids?"

She helps me set up in a back room with layered drop-cloths we fan out across the floor. The man wearing gold rings brings in easels with small blank canvases, shrink-wrapped and purchased from the dollar store. I haven't painted in years, but this is important to Alice, so it's important to me. It helps thicken my reality. We're on the ground floor, and I keep looking out the windows for Alice.

"Thank you so much for doing this," she says squeezing my arm.

But the painting class isn't for the kids, it's for the refugee men who don't have anything to do after working on their resumes. The kids have a structured program today because it's Monday. Every thirty minutes is allotted for and today is a special guest – the man with the gold rings. Volunteers are on strict regulated hours, and my dropping by like this has thrown things off. So when Alice tells the Syrian men, most huddled in a side room playing cards directly across from the room I'm in that I'll "do some art with them" they shrug, stand slowly, and enter the room.

It's obvious this situation calls for the professional, conference call version of myself. But it's been so long. I'm still checking the windows for Alice. She has to be gone by now, enough time has passed, I have done everything required. The men from the burning gas station are here, they nudge each other simultaneously while glaring at me and picking lint from the drop-cloths.

In my professional voice I say art produces compassion, so Alice, in the hall, can hear me. This is the version she fell in love with, so that's who I'm going to be. It's not my fault things changed. It's not my fault I became a different version from what I was supposed to be. I just couldn't figure out how to live.

I paint a sloppy thunderstorm with a green field and continue discussing the benefits of art in my professional voice. I combine the old me and the new, and the me thinking about Alice being home and Alice being here. Life is vicious. Life is sweet. Alice checks in then walks down the hall calling names – Amena, Mohammed, Tarek, Kamar, Uri. I'm doing a pretty good job painting this rain.

But I lecture the refugees. I tell them one belief is that art should be the center of our lives, we could work from the center of art to better understand our humanity. No one says anything. I even moved myself. I say that science and business and economics have failed us. Time we try something else and art has been waiting. As I paint, I quote Matisse, "Creativity takes courage," the old me flooding back over me, exciting me. "An artist can show things that other people are scared of expressing," Louise Bourgeois. I add stars and a constellation in the top right corner, it doesn't make sense, but I love it. "Everything you can imagine is real," Picasso.

Completing my first painting in years, I say a study showed a higher level of empathy in children when they grew up studying art. Adding one last drop of rain to the canvas, and a tiny black hole in the clouds, I'm proud of myself. I've needed this and now I've shared it with those in need.

"Fuck you," someone says from the back of the room.

I turn and face the small crowd, feel light-headed with nothing to grip onto.

Another voice from the middle: "Big bullshit."

Everyone is standing.

"Wait," I say desperately, "I'm trying to help."

A man in a black cap worn low across his eyes, he's all chin and black mustache, steps forward like he's going to hit me. "You don't," he says.

Everyone is leaving the room.

"What is it?" The black cap gestures vaguely toward the painting. He taps the painting with his knuckles like knocking on a door. "See? Does nothing."

I'm left alone with the realization that what my reality is – divorced, dead Rudy, dead Elderly, the office life, a retirement waiting after I've lived my best years – is too strong. I want to apologize, but Alice comes into the room.

I tell her the painting idea didn't go too well, they didn't like my tone. She says it's okay, slightly defeated, says they've had a long day, jobs aren't happening because, "A-ville." She adds they have very little chance of employment. So day and night they sit around RISSE, praying. Some have even considered returning home where they feel it's safer. She shakes her head at this idea. The painting idea was a bad idea.

"I'll finish up here. Be over at five," she says into my ear, giving me a hug. I don't have the chance or the guts to tell her that's also a bad idea.

At home I record a video of Alice, and on the replay see a wavering oval of air, a portal-shaped glistening suspended over the couch. I try and show her and she runs into the bedroom. Outside it's starting to rain so the men in the neighborhood are looking up at the sky.

One thing I've brought from the office, previously instructed to keep from the home after my gate opened, is the training manual and Dorian's research paper. I read from them in my professional voice, following Alice into the bedroom as her limbs flicker from cigarette ash to the gray of storm clouds.

She runs back past me, down the hall, past where we were once Leg Wobble Man together, and into the front room again. She has nowhere to go. I tell her again she isn't real. I tell her again this will not last. I go back through the rules as quickly as possible. I start to cry when she resembles fog settling against the door.

One of the men outside is setting-off fireworks in the rain. Through the windows an umbrella of gold sparks is coming down over the street. That's the only legislation I know the Leaders have ever passed – making fireworks legal again. Their retirement package is sickening. They only need ten years to retire, so all across America ex-Leaders are just relaxing, drinking Arnold Palmers, driving golf carts, signing checks on granite countertops.

Alice is still able to stand, even in her current form, and runs to the kitchen. She leaves behind a damp trail. I break more rules. Destroying her, I have this song stuck in my head. The lyrics were written on orange construction paper, stuck on my bedroom wall, each corner with layers of masking tape:

> All together now
> Raise your voices to the sky
> Magic will happen here somehow
> If we're all together now

Mom loved this song. She hummed it during naps. After she woke and moved to the couch I'd make her bed. I can still smell those sheets, see her socks balled-up at the end of the bed. But there's no reason why this song should be in my head now besides that there's no reason to the world. Stuff just enters your head and you have no control over it. I can't find Alice.

She appears in the backyard rubbing her arms. In the wind she turns off and on. I'm waiting for something to happen, her final disappearance, a dramatic puddle of Alice into the soil. She walks to the backdoor. I hear it open as I prepare myself to break more rules. But she doesn't come up the back stairs, she goes down.

The basement is one long and wide room, the entire size of my first floor apartment. There isn't much in here. Dangling lightbulbs, cobwebs between the wooden beams, and a dirt floor with a washer and dryer topped in purple lint. The landlord uses the space to store paint cans, random tools, and bargain priced items from Home Depot. I'm forced to walk hunchback-style because of the low ceilings, looking for Alice.

"Hello?"

I wanted to be a good person. I wanted a simple life. Don't blame me for how life worked out, blame time, blame time, blame time. See? A year is just a lap around the sun. The moon has moves but the stars can't tell you anything.

I slowly walk forward, calling for Alice. The landlord's work bench contains many saws and I run my finger through a clump of sawdust.

Alice, or at least a shape resembling a person, runs into the further dark, toward the far back corners of the basement.

I break apart Alice, speaking into the dark how she isn't real, telling her she's an illusion who can't survive, controlling the space, controlling my life, taking more pictures (I glance down, all black), threatening to leave her down here forever, killing her.

I hear her whimpering as I approach her, walking past unwrapped plumbing parts the landlord has stored against the wall.

I dip under a rusty metal beam. At the end of the basement Alice is kneeling in the corner, becoming smaller against the concrete and dirt.

One final time I work my way through the list.

*All together now…*

Alice becomes an oval shaped portal.

Fog.

White smoke translucent with stars.

A constellation of a woman suspended in the sky.

Mist withdrawing into a black hole.

A distant voice.

Now gone.

I move my hand through the air in front of me and it's a coincidence I make the shape of a cross. I look down. My fingertips are wet. On the dirt floor there's a dampness, a sweet smell, one strand of hair.

Upstairs, someone is knocking. Where I am in the basement, Alice is directly above.

This is my life. A seamless transition from one Alice to another as I open the door. Alice is coming into the apartment for the first time since leaving the apartment. Maybe being alive isn't so cruel. Maybe everyone comes back to you.

# JULY 4

Thousands tilt their heads backwards at the first firework. America is always in celebration mode. Even in the bleakest of times we'll fly our flags and light up the sky. Wearing shorts in the colors of the flag while getting drunk doesn't have to be mocked, maybe it just feels right.

I'm one of the few walking from the celebration. I don't really care about fireworks, but Mom and Dad did, we never missed a Fourth, and nearing forty years old, I haven't missed one either.

Last night Alice and I had dinner together and it was amazing. I had nothing prepared so I made grilled cheese sandwiches. Again? Again. I thought about making eggs but didn't want to mess them up.

Watching her move around the apartment I thought she would disappear or ask where Alice was. But she seemed calm, back in the apartment, after so long. She talked about how lonely she was in Chicago, how I would like it there so much more than A-ville.

"Chicago is basically a much bigger and better version," she said.

"But in Illinois."

I flipped a sandwich and Alice smiled. "Right," she agreed, "but in Illinois."

Just outside where the plaza ends, a man with a shaved head, dressed in red and black is handing out little wooden crosses, and I want to avoid him, I tell myself to avoid him, but for some reason I take the cross and thank him. I don't have time for this. I have to get home. I have a life to live. Alice is with the refugees now, but I'm going to see her later.

"Let me ask you something," says The Cross Man. "My brother, are you happy?"

"It's not part of the deal," I say flippantly, "but I'm good today."

"Belief in God will lead you to wonderful places," says The Cross Man, leaping forward to give a couple on their way to the plaza two crosses. They are so innocent, the wooden crosses, that everyone who is handed one, takes one.

"Not interested in heaven?" He has a spider web tattoo covering his elbow. On his wrist ORION with no surrounding stars. "How can you not be interested in the next level?"

"The constellation," I say, pointing to his wrist.

"Not exactly," he replies.

Last night I asked if she would ever move back to A-ville and she gave me a look, that Alice look, ugh, crushes me. When she flipped the question, would I ever move to Chicago, you know what the first thing I thought was? My retirement. Twenty more years isn't that long if you fracture it, year by year, month by month. Twenty Christmas days. Twenty laps around the sun. I told all this to Alice and she stared at her lap. I said she should consider moving to A-ville, but she didn't respond. I still think I can convince her.

The fireworks give an increased light to the sky, but then it's dark again. And because the fireworks are sounding off on the plaza, the echoing off the agency buildings is deafening. Parents with infants are running from the blasts. Walls of white light flash on the marble facades. If you didn't know it was a fireworks display you would assume something was wrong. But nothing is wrong. Everything feels hopeful. Alice just needs to decide to be with me.

"You won't be reunited with anyone you love," continues The Cross Man. "My brother, join our path," he pleads, his voice soft and comforting. He hands me a pamphlet with an iron cross on the cover. He laughs when I refuse to take it.

Something else about last night: I couldn't stop thinking about PER Alice. I knew she was gone, but part of me felt like she was still down there, in the basement, breathing. Breaking the rules, she talked about our trip to the castle, saying she wanted to go back, telling me to stop, until she stopped. But that breathing. I swear I could hear it rising through the floorboards while sitting on the couch with Alice.

The Cross Man yells about heaven and salvation, shielding babies from Satan, the time is now to be saved. There's a carnival approach to what he's saying to no one in particular, but it feels like his yelling is directed at me, not those running around me. The faster I walk away the louder he becomes.

In last night's dream I was escaping. I don't know what exactly, but I was in the Pontiac and Elderly was driving. Police sirens were flashing behind us. That wasn't what we were escaping from, something else was lurking its way toward us.

Elderly had this big lunatic grin on his face, hunched over the wheel, pedal to the floor. The road was desert but smooth as pavement. I was in the back seat with some version of Alice, but it looked like we were in bed, how we slept together wrapped around each other in the twilight-dark. It must have been blistering hot because we wore strips of clothing. All the windows were down. Alice whispered something in my ear that made me sit up. Through the windshield the sky was a screen with a waterfall pouring out of it and Dorian was beneath it, waving. And as we sped away from the sirens and at that sky Rudy in the passenger seat put his head out the window, blood-tongue hanging loose like it was meant to. Alice squeezed my hand as we drove into outstretched arms.

# ACKNOWLEDGMENTS

Thank you Giancarlo DiTrapano, Rebekah Bergman,
Adam Robinson, and Sarah Bowlin.

Shane Jones is the author of three previous novels: *Light Boxes, Daniel Fights a Hurricane*, and *Crystal Eaters*. He lives in Troy, NY.